# It's Only Make Believe

## IONA ROSE

# Author's Note

Hey there!

Thank you for choosing my book. I sure hope that you love it. I'd hate to part ways once you're done though. So how about we stay in touch?

My newsletter is a great way to discover more about me and my books. Where you'll find frequent exclusive give-aways, sneak previews of new releases and be first to see new cover reveals.

And as a HUGE thank you for joining, you'll receive a FREE book on me!

With love,

Iona

Get Your FREE Book Here:
https://dl.bookfunnel.com/v9yit8b3f7

# *Prologue*

## TIA

I take one final glance at the now empty dorm room behind me. All that remains are two empty desks, two chairs and two stripped beds. The posters are gone, the personal effects, the laptops and everything that made the dorm room ours. I look at Louisa and give her a sad smile.

"I can't believe it's over," I say.

"I know," she replies. "It's the end of an era. Four years sharing a room, and we didn't want to kill each other once."

"That in itself feels like more of an achievement than our degrees," I joke.

Louisa laughs and nods in agreement. She links her hand through my arm, careful not to dislodge the box I'm carrying. All of Louisa's stuff is already packed into the trunk of her car and this is the last of mine, the rest of it has also been put away in the trunk of my own car.

"Let's grab lunch before we go," Louisa says, and I nod my agreement gratefully.

I know I have to leave campus, and I know I should be

excited to start the rest of my life, but I'm not. Unlike Louisa, who has a family to go home to, I have nothing. My mom died when I was in my first year of college and I'm an only child. Her parents died long ago, and my dad has never been a part of my life. The only thing that man gave me is a surname, something I would have been just as happy to get from my mom. I feel kind of lost now that my final year of college is over if I'm honest, and although having lunch with Louisa will only add an extra hour or so to my time here, I'm still glad for the reprieve.

We walk to my car so I can put my last box in the trunk and then we head to the student canteen where I order a cheeseburger and fries with a soda and Louisa gets a chilli dog with fries and a carton of juice. We pay for our food and find a table and begin eating.

"Do we have to be all grown up now and stop eating junk food after today," I say, trying to keep the mood light.

Louisa snorts out a laugh. "I hope not," she says.

We lapse back into silence, a comfortable silence, the kind that only true friends or soulmates can experience without feeling awkward.

"So, what now?" Louisa asks me after a few more bites of her chili dog and a small handful of fries.

We've had this conversation several times leading up to the end of the year and I have always bluffed my way through it saying I haven't decided yet, or I have a few options I'm considering. For the first time, I tell her the sad truth.

"I have no idea," I say. "I mean I guess I'll stay here in New York. I have a hotel booked for tonight and I'll have to try and find an apartment and a job."

"You don't have anything lined up?" Louisa asks and I shake my head. "So why stay here in a city you no longer love? You have no one here anymore."

"Thanks for the reminder," I say.

"I didn't mean it like that. I meant come to Chicago. It's way cheaper to get an apartment there than here and there are tons of internships in IT," she says. "You can stay with us until you can rent an apartment."

I think about it for a moment. I have stayed with the Sanchez family a few times in the holidays, and they are lovely, welcoming people and I love staying with them. But if I do this, I will have to find an apartment quickly. I don't want them to think I'm taking their kindness for granted. Do I want this though? I think for a moment longer and I realize that I can't think of a single reason not to do it. I grin at Louisa.

"OK. Chicago it is," I say.

"Correct answer. But first, let's take advantage of that hotel room you have booked and have one last night in New York," Louisa says with a grin, and I nod, my own grin spreading across my face as I feel a weight lifting from my shoulders.

# CHAPTER
*One*

## LUKE

I walk away from my car, where it's parked in my reserved parking space, and I head to the entrance of the headquarters of Sold, an online auction website that I am the CEO of. I started Sold at just the right time and it took off more than I had ever even dared to dream it would, and the company is now worth over a billion dollars.

I enter the lobby and the receptionist greets me. I return the greeting and head to the elevator. The first five floors of the building belong to Sold and I ride up to the fifth floor where my office is. The lobby and elevator car are busy as it's that time of the morning where the majority of people are coming in to work. I greet and am greeted by some employees and a few people from other firms who I'm now on speaking terms with after seeing them around the building so often.

The elevator pings to a stop on the fifth floor and I get out of it and head along the hallway to my office.

"Morning Mel," I say as I duck my head around my PA's door. "Any messages?"

"Morning," Mel replies. "Only one important one. Enrique Sanchez called. He requested you call him back. He said it's urgent."

"Thanks Mel," I say, and I continue on to my office, wondering what Enrique might want that is so urgent.

Enrique Sanchez is the highest shareholder in Sold after me and he's the chairman of the board of directors. He very rarely interferes in the day to day running of the business, and it's unusual for him to call me like this out of the blue.

I get to my office, go inside and take my jacket off. I take my cell phone from the pocket and then hang it on one of the coat hooks on the wall behind my door. I move across my spacious office and sit down behind the large oak desk. I fire up my computer out of habit because usually my first task is checking the stock value of the company, but today, my first task is calling Enrique back.

I scroll through my cell phone and find his number which I type into my office phone. I put my cell phone in my top drawer while I listen to the ringing sound down my ear. I don't have long to wait before Enrique answers my call with a gruff hello.

"Enrique? Hi, it's Luke Jackson returning your call," I say.

"Ah. Good morning, Luke. How are you?" he asks. His words carry the slightest hint of his Spanish accent, but he speaks English as well as anyone I've ever met.

"I'm good thanks. How are you?" I ask.

His voice is giving nothing away as to the reason for his call, although he doesn't sound pissed off, so I guess that's a good thing.

"I'll be better in a moment if you agree to do me a small personal favor," he says.

"Go on," I say.

I'm not stupid enough to agree to the favor before I know what it is, but I will certainly hear him out, and if it's something I can do, I will do it. Enrique holds a lot of sway when it comes to company votes and a lot of the smaller shareholders just vote whichever way he does, so it's always a good idea to keep him on my side.

"I need you to give my daughter, Louisa, an internship," Enrique says.

My heart sinks at his words. When he said a personal favor, I thought maybe he wanted to borrow my driver for a few days, or something like that. Not something that involves the company. I want to help Enrique, but I won't let the company carry dead weight. My employees have enough to do at the moment, especially now that Diane has left the web development team, and the last thing the staff needs is to have to babysit Enrique's daughter. He must sense some of my thoughts from my silence, because he goes on before I get a chance to say no.

"Although I'm asking as a favor, Louisa is qualified. She's just graduated from NYU with a degree in web development and she has an offer from a tech company here, but one of the conditions of employment is that she has three months experience," Enrique says.

That definitely changes things slightly and I find myself agreeing to take Louisa on. She sounds like she will help the web development team rather than get in the way and it's a nice solution to our short staff problem. It also means I have three months to find a permanent replacement for Diane instead of having to rush into taking the first person who fits the bill.

"I won't ask my daughter to do something I wouldn't do myself, so the internship can't be unpaid," Enrique says to me. "But I understand from a business standpoint that the company needs to do that. I will pay Louisa a wage, but she needs to be under the impression it comes from the company. She knows better than to discuss salary with other employees so it's not like anyone will know."

"Ok," I agree.

"And lastly. Don't treat her like my daughter. Treat her like any other intern. Louisa is a bright girl, and I'm confident she can do anything you ask of her, but she's … er…. lazy is the wrong word. Unmotivated I think is maybe better," Enrique says. "I hate to use the word spoiled or entitled, but she seems to think she can lie about the experience needed and the company won't find out. Honestly, I don't think she cares much if they do. She seems to think she can coast through life on my dime and it's time for her to see that's not going to wash anymore."

He might not like the words spoiled or entitled, but it doesn't change the fact that based on the description he has just given me, his daughter is definitely one of those things. Maybe even both.

"So, you're sending me a lazy, entitled girl who technically doesn't need a job. Thanks for that," I say, half joking. "I'm sure she'll be a valuable asset."

Enrique laughs.

"Something like that. But as I said, she's a bright girl and I have no doubt that underneath that spoiled exterior, there's a woman who can make it in this field or any other field she chooses. I think she just needs to experience the real world a little bit more, you know, where she is answerable to someone other than her mom and me and is expected to perform just like everyone else," Enrique says.

"Don't worry," I say. "I'll kick her ass and make her employable."

"That's what I wanted to hear. Thanks Luke. I owe you one. I'll tell her she starts at nine am sharp on Monday morning," Enrique says.

I agree and he hangs up. I replace the receiver and sit for a moment. I hope I can keep the promise I've just made, because having Enrique owe me one is exactly what I need right now, because I have a big idea that I'm working on and it will be ready to pitch to the board by the end of the year, and I really want Enrique's support on it.

# CHAPTER
## *Two*

**TIA**

Louisa stands up as I walk across the bar towards her. I reach the table, and we hug.

"I'm so sorry I'm late," I say as we sit down. "Honestly, I know like two people in Chicago, and I'm late to meet one of them because the other one called, and I lost track of time."

Louisa wrinkles her nose.

"You're not seriously considering getting back with Justin, are you?" Louisa asks.

I shake my head.

"No. As a couple we just didn't work, there was no chemistry between us. But we got along well enough and there's no harm in being friends. And besides, in a brand new city, I'm hardly in a place to turn my back on someone I actually know," I tell her.

"I still think it's creepy that he followed you here," Louisa says.

I roll my eyes.

"For the fiftieth time, he didn't follow me here. He took a job offer here before he even knew I was coming here. Hell, it was before I had even decided to come here," I say.

"That's what he tells you," Louisa says. "But is it the truth?"

I roll my eyes again and Louisa takes the hint and laughs and pushes a glass of rose wine towards me.

"Forget Justin, drink up," she says.

I pick up the glass and take a big sip and moan my appreciation when the cold sweetness of the wine runs over my tongue. I swallow my first mouthful and take another drink.

"You look like you needed that," Louisa says.

"I did," I agree. "Job hunting is thirsty work. Especially when there are so few options. I mean don't get me wrong, there are tons of jobs I could do, but I don't want to stack shelves or fold clothes. I want something actually related to my degree. There's just nothing. Well, there are unpaid internships of course but I need money. I'm starting to think I'm going to have to take an unpaid internship and then wait tables or tend bar or something on evenings and weekends."

"Funny you should say that" Louisa says. "I actually have something I thought you might be interested in."

I feel my interest being piqued and I sit up straighter and look at Louisa, waiting for her to go on. I'm struck, certainly not for the first time, and probably not for the last time, how pretty Louisa is. She has caramel crème colored skin with dark brown eyes and dark brown curls. She has a lovely, curvaceous figure, and she is as beautiful inside as she is outside. I still sometimes have to pinch myself to believe that she chose me, Tia Lake, a self-confessed nobody, to be her best friend at college and now beyond.

"Earth calling," Louisa says, and I snap back to attention.

"Sorry," I say. "I was miles away."

Louisa laughs.

"Yeah, I saw," she says. "I was just saying not to get too excited about the proposal I have for you. It's paid work, but it's only an internship so the pay isn't fantastic, but ..."

"But it'll give me experience that will give me a chance at getting a foot in the door somewhere," I finish for her. "And might mean I don't have to work a second job too."

"Exactly," Louisa agrees. "So, you're interested then?"

I nod.

"Yes," I say. "Let me just go and grab us some more drinks and then I want to hear all about it."

I get up and head for the bar before Louisa can object. It's no secret that I'm not exactly drowning in money. In fact, I have enough in my bank account for like two months of rent and bills and when that's gone, I have nothing. Louisa on the other hand comes from money and while her father is getting a bit pissed off with her not working by all accounts, she still isn't going to be homeless or have to choose between heating and food any time soon. For that reason, Louisa is more than happy to pay on nights out, but I like to be able to pay my way. I love Louisa and I know her offer comes from a place of her love for me, but I want to be on equal footing, not her little charity case that she drags out when she needs an excuse to feel good about herself. I know that's not fair, but it's how I feel, and I can't help it.

I get served with two Aperol Spritz cocktails and go back to the table. I set one down in front of Louisa and she nods her head in approval.

"Nice," she says after a sip. "So, this internship. It's with a big tech company and it will be mostly working with the web development team from what I understand about it, although obviously it's an internship so you'll probably have to do some dog's body work as well."

"Yeah, I would expect that," I agree. "What's the catch."

"Who said there was going to be a catch?" Louisa says.

Her innocent look only convinces me that there's a catch and that it's a big one. I don't answer and she sighs. "Fine. There is a catch. But it's a teeny tiny one. You have to pretend to be me."

I look at gorgeous, Latina Louisa and then down at myself. I'm the picture someone would paint if they were asked to draw a person who was the opposite to Louisa. Firstly, I am so white, milk feels sorry for me. My hair is a light blonde, a natural shade that almost no one believes is natural, and my eyes are bright blue. Where Louisa is short and curvy, I'm tall and willowy. I definitely got my mom's Scandinavian looks.

"Who the hell is going to believe I am you?" I say.

"No one at the company has seen me," Louisa says. "There's no reason why they won't. And this way, we both win. You will get paid for doing the sort of thing you want to do, and I will get my father off my back because he will think I'm doing the internship. And the reference at the end can easily be used by both of us, we just need to make a copy and change the name."

I can feel myself on the verge of saying yes, although it still feels like I'm not getting the whole story.

"It pays eight hundred dollars a week after deductions," Louisa says.

"Ok. I'm in," I say.

Fuck the catch. That will pay for my rent which is almost fifteen hundred dollars a month – a bargain for a one-bedroom apartment in downtown Chicago I am assured by Louisa – and leave me with enough left over for utilities, food, and maybe even a bit of a social life.

"Congratulations on the new job," Louisa grins. "You start at nine o'clock on Monday morning. I'll text you the address and the details. I'd say don't be late, but you're meant to be me, so feel free."

She laughs and I roll my eyes and laugh with her. When we stop laughing, Louisa goes to the bar and this time, we're drinking something called a Mellow Marshmallow. It's sweet and a bit coconutty and I like it. While she was gone, a question came to my mind. I'm about to ask it, although I'm not sure I really want to know the answer.

"Louisa, I have to ask. This internship. It's paid which is practically unheard of. Even the odd paid internship I've heard of pays closer to six hundred dollars a week and this is eight hundred dollars after deductions. Is there something I should know?" I ask.

"Well, now that you mention it, there was something about disposing of dead bodies, but it's only now and again, and you probably won't have to do more than one or two," Louisa says with a grin.

I laugh and shake my head, and she turns serious again and shrugs one shoulder.

"I assume they are paying a bit more than average because they think it's actually going to be me and my dad is on the board of directors," Louisa says.

My mouth drops open. I think I would have preferred the first explanation. There's no way I can take this job now. It explains why Louisa was careful not to mention the name of the company. I didn't notice at the time, but I do now. If she had mentioned it was Sold sooner, it would have been an instant no from me. I have already purposely avoided looking for any positions at the company after learning Enrique is on the board because I didn't want it to come out that I knew his daughter, and have it look like that's why I got the job. Now, she's suggesting I should pretend to be her there. How could that ever work?

"I'm out," I say. "You told me no one at the company knew what you looked like. I think your dad might know your face. And he knows me too."

"That's the beauty of it. He and my mom leave tomorrow for a cruise around Europe. The internship will be done by the time they return. My dad will hear how wonderful I was, because obviously it's you and you rock, and you will have some high powered job by then," Louisa says.

"I don't know," I say, looking down into my almost empty glass.

"Look at it this way. You pretending to be me isn't a crime. The worst thing that can happen if it does come out, is my dad will be pissed at me, which he is right now anyway and you'll get fired, meaning you won't have a job, which you don't right now anyway. See what I mean? In the worst case scenario, things go back to how they are right now, that's it. And in every other scenario, everything gets one hundred percent better for both of us," Louisa says.

She grins at me, nodding her head ever so slightly as I think. I don't even know why I'm thinking about it. Or at least pretending to be. The money sold me, but I can never say no to Louisa anyway, although this is the first one of her schemes or ideas that I can see seriously backfiring on us. But fuck it. I am actually going to give this a shot.

"Nine o' clock Monday morning. Sold, here I come," I say.

Louisa whoops and then drains her drink and motions for me to do the same. I finish it up and Louisa gets up, pulling me up with her and leading me out of the bar.

"But Monday at nine o'clock is almost thirty six hours away. So, let's go to a club and dance and drink and celebrate your new job."

"That is the best idea you've had in ages," I say with a grin, and I turn towards the road and flag down a passing cab, and we get in it to go to the club.

# CHAPTER
## *Three*

## LUKE

It's ten to nine on Monday morning and I'm waiting for Enrique's daughter to come to my office which is where she was told to go in the brief I sent her. I hope she isn't late, because that's a really bad start and although I have promised Enrique that I will ride her hard, and I meant it, I don't really want to have to sack her before we have even said hello. I'm pretty sure that wasn't Enrique's aim either.

I've already decided that for at least this week, Louisa will be working directly under me. I won't let her loose in the web development team until she has proven herself. I want to be able to give them someone who will help them, not a lazy spoiled brat who will slow things down for them.

It's eight minutes to nine when there's a quiet knock on my office door.

"Come in," I call.

The door opens and a beautiful blonde woman steps in. She's tall, about five foot eight or five foot nine, and she is slim to the point of her sleek body being almost androgynous looking, although there is nothing androgynous about her face. She is stunning, with bright, ice blue eyes that I feel like I could drown in and long, white-blonde hair. I have no idea who she is or why she's here, but she has certainly brightened up my morning.

"Can I help you?" I say after a pause when it's clear that she isn't going to speak first.

"I'm meant to be starting work here today. I'm Louisa Sanchez," the beautiful blonde says.

I try to hide my surprise. She is the last thing I expected when I pictured Enrique's daughter. I thought she would have black hair and olive skin. In short, I didn't expect her to look like a damned Viking queen like this woman before me does. I realize I have failed to hide my shock when she smiles at me.

"I take after my mom. She's Swedish," she says.

That should clear things up, but it doesn't. I've met Enrique's wife and she's Latina too. I guess Louisa must be Enrique's child from a previous marriage, but no, I have met her older sister too, who is also Latina. Could she be Enrique's love child or something? I tell myself to get a grip. She could be adopted or anything. And whatever it is, it's definitely none of my business.

I stand up, smile, and walk towards her with my hand extended.

"I'm Luke. Luke Jackson," I say.

She smiles back and gives me a nice firm handshake.

"It's a pleasure to meet you Mr. Jackson," she says.

"Oh, just Luke please," I say. "Being called Mr. Jackson makes me feel like I should be twice my age."

She laughs and it's a pretty, feminine sound. God she's gorgeous. She's actually the first woman in ages who has captured my attention in this way, who I feel like I want to get to know. And who I definitely want to be inside of. Typical she has to be a board member's daughter, and therefore off limits to me, especially while she's working for me.

I gesture to the seat opposite mine, and she sits down, and I go to my own seat and sit behind my desk. I wipe my suddenly sweaty palms on my knees and then I place my hands on my desk. I tell myself to get a grip. It's not like I haven't seen a beautiful woman before.

"Tell me about your degree and your experience," I say.

"My degree covered the basics in most areas of IT, but it's main focus and my main area of expertise was web development. I did several placements throughout my degree where I designed and built websites, apps, that kind of thing," she says. "And I also did a bit of web building and maintenance prior to going to college."

I nod.

"Ok," I say. "Now keep in mind that this position is an internship, and you will learn as you go. Sitting through lectures and actually doing the work are often very different things and there's no shame in admitting it if there's something that comes up that you don't know or aren't sure about."

Louisa nods her agreement. So far, she's surprisingly enthusiastic in her approach and she isn't coming over as entitled or spoiled, but to be fair, I haven't actually asked her to do anything except sit down and talk about herself yet.

"Until I think you're ready to get into that side of things, I have some tasks for you to complete. The first thing you need to know and remember is Americano with milk and two sugars," I tell Louisa.

I wait for some sarcastic comment about her not being a barista or a waitress or a servant or something like that, but she just nods her head.

"Noted," she says. "For the record, mine is a caramel macchiato."

"I can think of no circumstances where I will need to know that, but thanks for the information," I say. I stand up and Louisa follows suit. "I'm going to introduce you to my personal assistant. She will show you around and show you where you will be working. Once that's done, come back here and I will give you your first task."

I head out of the office without looking back to make sure Louisa is following me. I hear her footsteps behind me which confirms she actually is. I take her to Mel's office and tap on the door and go inside when she calls out to come in.

"Louisa, this is Mel Rose, my personal assistant and general superwoman. Mel, this is Louisa Sanchez, the new intern and general dog's body I told you was starting today. Can you give her the tour, get her set up on the systems, all of that kind of thing?" I say.

Mel nods her head although she is looking at me kind of strangely. I know why. It's the dog's body comment. Something I would never normally say about a new intern, especially not in front of them, not even as a joke. I felt Louisa bristle beside me at my words too, but to her credit, she didn't comment on them. Maybe her mean girl side will come out more with Mel, someone she probably thinks is beneath her if she's so entitled, rather than with me, her boss. If it does, she will be sorry, because Mel is one of my most valued employees and if this jumped up intern upsets her, there will be hell to pay.

# CHAPTER
## *Four*

## TIA

This morning has been a roller coaster ride already and it's not even a quarter past nine in the morning yet. I came in less than a half an hour ago – it feels like so much longer than that - and met my boss, Luke. He's younger than I thought he would be, definitely not out of his twenties. And he is smoking hot, although he's an asshole to boot, so good looking or not, at least I don't fancy him. No, really, I don't.

I used my coffee joke, where I tell the boss my order when he tells me his, and I have found that in most of my work experience placements throughout college that all of them have laughed. The better ones actually bought me a coffee at some point. Luke just basically told me I wasn't important enough for him to need to know that about me. And then the way he described me as a general dog's body to Mel made me want to punch him. I did see Mel look briefly shocked before she covered the expression with a more neutral look and that definitely made me lean towards liking her. She's almost certainly loyal to Luke, but she isn't one of those mindless employees that don't have their own thoughts and opinions.

She's almost as tall as me, and she has black skin and black hair that she wears in a funky updo. She's really pretty, with eyes of a golden shade that I would kill for. She looks sophisticated in her form fitting dress and bolero jacket, especially next to me in my black pants and white blouse. Could I have chosen anything more boring? I am going to have to up my fashion game here. At least it's not like the placement I went on where I wore a full skirt suit and smart blouse, only to find out the rest of the staff were wearing jeans and oversized hoodies and sneakers. At least my boring outfit doesn't stand out and make me look silly.

I'm glad when Luke leaves Mel's office and it's just the two of us. I feel some of the tension go out of my spine and Mel smiles at me warmly which helps too. I want to quiz her about Luke, about why he is being so mean to me for no reason, but I figure that even though she's being nice to me, her loyalties obviously lie with Luke and she's not going to bitch about him with me, and there's also the possibility anything I ask about him will get back to him, and I don't want him to think I even noticed he was being mean. I want him to just think I'm unaffected by him.

"Are you ready for the tour or do you need a moment first? It's a lot isn't it, that first few minutes in a new job," Mel says.

"It is," I agree. "But I'm ok. I'm ready for the tour."

Mel nods her head, and I follow her out of her office, down the hallway and to the elevator car. Mel presses the call button, and we wait. I hear the rattling sound of the car getting into motion and soon enough, the doors ping open, and we get into the elevator.

"You've obviously seen the lobby and met Elenor, the receptionist there?" Mel says, and I nod.

"Elenor introduced herself to me when I told her who I was and why I'm here," I confirm. "She seems nice."

"She is, but seeing as you've already met her, there's not much else to see on the ground floor, so let's start on the next floor up then," she says and she reaches out a perfectly manicured, purple colored nail and presses the button marked one. We reach the floor and get out of the elevator. This floor is very different from the fifth floor. Where that floor has a long corridor and lots of offices, this floor is mostly an open plan with people working in cubicles alongside each other. Mel points to the right. "That's the customer services team." Then she points to the left. "And that's the sales team. Half of them sell advertising slots on the site and the other half try to boost up the number of site users we have. To be honest, I don't think you'll have much need to be down here unless you want to try your hand at sales?"

"God no," I say with a shudder and Mel laughs.

"My feelings exactly," she says.

Mel leads me back to the elevator and we get in and go up one floor. This floor is more like the fifth floor with individual rooms, although the rooms here are larger, and each have multiple people working in them. Mel leads me to the first door, and we go in.

"This is the HR department," Mel says. She leads me over to a desk where a woman smiles a greeting at us. "Susan Hall, Louisa Sanchez, our new intern." I smile and Susan and I shake hands and exchange pleasantries. "I'm sure you won't need to, but if you do ever need to lodge a formal complaint, Susan is your point of contact."

"I'm sure I won't need to lodge a complaint," I agree. "Unless of course I don't get long enough lunch breaks."

I risk another joke, smiling to show it's definitely a joke and this one pays off. Both Mel and Susan laugh.

"You will get long enough, as long as five minutes at your

desk, eating with one hand and typing with the other one is enough," Mel says.

"Obviously," I agree and the three of us laugh some more and then Mel leads me out of the room and to the next one. "This here is the payroll department. I'll show you later how to complete your time sheets and when and where to send them to."

We head back to the elevator, and we go to floor three.

The first part of the hallway shows a decent sized room with two men working in it, beside a huge, glass walled room filled with servers.

"That's our IT department," Mel says. "Obviously everyone here is pretty tech savvy, but these guys know more about the workings of computers than anyone, and if there is a problem with any computer that you can't fix, call down to them. They also set up new employees on the systems and stuff, which again, I will go through with you later."

We are still walking, and the corridor opens out to a large open space where five people sit around a good sized pod of desks with dividers between them that are low enough to still be able to speak to each other. One desk is empty.

"This here is the web development team. I believe that's your main focus?" Mel says. I nod, and she smiles. "Well, that empty desk might become yours if you can prove yourself."

"I really hope so," I reply.

Mel introduces me to the team. I know I will never remember all of their names, but it's still nice to be introduced to them. They seem like a friendly enough bunch, and I definitely think I would fit in here with these people. When we've chatted for a while about my degree and what they are working on and a few other things, Mel clears her throat.

"I think it's time for us to head back up," she says.

"Oh, sure, sorry," I reply.

"It's ok," she says, and we say our goodbyes and she leads

me back to the elevator. She presses the button for the fifth floor. "The fourth floor is all conference rooms where we mostly hold team meetings, but sometimes potential advertisers and what not want to come in and have meetings. That all takes place there. I won't show you yet because there's really nothing to see except a bunch of empty rooms. There will be a meeting later on though so you will see the conference rooms then and at least now you know where to find them."

We get back onto the fifth floor and Mel walks over to a desk that was previously empty but now has a woman sitting behind it.

"Rachel, this is Louisa, our new intern. Louisa, this is Rachel Whittington, Luke's personal receptionist," Mel says.

Rachel and I greet each other and then Mel continues down the hallway with me behind her. She points to a few closed doors as we pass them.

"That's the men's bathroom, and that's the ladies' bathroom for this floor," she says. "And that there is the breakroom, and beside it, the kitchen. There's a fridge, coffee machine, and microwave in the break room for the use of staff. Please don't use the kitchen for personal use."

"Ok," I quickly agree.

"That's the mail room for our floor and that one there is for photocopying, scanning and shredding. We also keep all of our current files in there. And that one is where all of the old files are archived," Mel goes on, pointing at more doors.

Finally, Mel takes me to one of the last doors before we reach Luke's office. It's directly opposite Mel's office. She opens the door, and I'm ushered inside of a room that is basically a storage cupboard, but instead of supplies, there's a desk and a chair crammed into the room. On the desk is a computer and a telephone, plus two empty trays marked in and out. The walls are grey, and the paintwork is white. A small window lends some light to the room. It's tiny but functional and as an intern I'm just happy to have an office at all.

"This is where you'll be based until Luke says otherwise," Mel tells me.

I look around again, more critical this time now that Mel has made it sound like I could be here for a long time. It's still tiny -there's no getting around that - but the décor looks new and fresh and it's not like I'm wanting to host parties in the space. It's big enough for a desk and a chair and I can't see what else I might need at this point.

"Sit down and switch your computer on," Mel says.

I move around the desk with a small degree of difficulty. The real Louisa wouldn't have gotten through the gap without going up on her tippy toes, but I have no ass, so I manage it without too much contortionism. Just. I plonk down in the chair, waiting for it to break or something equally bad, but nothing happens, and I switch the computer on as Mel directed me to. Mel perches on the edge of the desk and points to a sheet of paper on the top of it. It should be in the in tray I can't help but think. Naturally, I choose not to point this out to Mel in case she is the one who left it there. Or worse, Luke left it there. I stop obsessing over the sheet and turn my attention back to Mel as she begins to speak again, pointing momentarily at the sheet again as she does.

"That's your logins for each system. Even if you don't know the system or how to work it yet, please enter each one and make sure the logins work. Don't do anything else. You will be shown how the systems work as and when you need them. You will also find details of how to get paid on the sheet. Once you have done that, you can go back to Luke and see what he wants you to do today," Mel says. "Do let me know if there are any issues."

"Got it," I say. "Thank you for the tour and for making me feel welcome."

Mel smiles at me and goes to leave. She stops at the door.

"If you want to impress Luke, don't go to his office without his coffee," she says.

I nod. I really don't like the idea of being the dog's body, but I know I have to suck it up and prove myself before I'm trusted with anything else. And at least there's a coffee machine. It's not like I have to do much, just put a cup beneath the spout and press a button. I'm sure I can manage that easily enough.

Mel leaves and I quickly go through the list in front of me and log in to each system. Each one works perfectly well and then I get to the bit about how to be paid. I go to the page on the company intranet that I'm directed to and download a timesheet. I need to fill it in every day and email it to the payroll department at the end of the week, which again, I'm sure I can manage. I set a reminder on my cell phone for Friday to send the time sheet just in case I forget all the same.

With all of that done, I go to the breakroom, grab a mug and put it beneath the spout on the coffee machine, and then I hit the button for an Americano. The machine rattles to life and while it makes and pours the coffee, I find the sugar and the milk. When the coffee is done, I add milk and two spoons of sugar. I give the drink a quick stir and then I rinse the spoon and return it to the drawer where I found it and then I head to Luke's office with the cup of coffee in my hand.

I take a deep breath to steady my nerves and then I knock on the door.

"Come in," Luke calls and I open the door and step into his office.

# CHAPTER
*Five*

## TIA

I am once again floored by how good looking this man is. He is at least six feet tall and while some people that tall look gangly, Luke isn't one of those people. He is toned and perfectly in proportion with himself. He has dark brown hair which he wears short around the sides and a bit longer on the top, and he has the most gorgeous green eyes. He has the classic chiselled cheekbones, and I'm sure that beneath the stubble he sports on his chin, his jawbone will be equally pleasing to the eye. But I don't fancy him. It's not an attraction to Luke that makes my palms sweaty and my mouth dry and it's certainly nothing to do with him that makes my pussy feel damp.

I walk towards the desk and put the cup down in front of him.

"Americano, milk, two sugars," I say.

"I don't remember asking for this," Luke replies.

"I can take it away if you don't want it," I say, forcing myself not to sound annoyed.

"No need for that," Luke says as though he's the one doing me the favor rather than the other way around. "I'll drink it."

Big of you, I think but don't say.

"I've had my tour, and I'm live on all of the systems," I say. "You said to come back and get my first task when that was done."

"Sit down," Luke says.

I'm glad he has finally invited me to sit down. Standing up, I didn't really know what to do with my hands, but I had a feeling if I had sat down without an invite, Luke would have had something to say about it and I wasn't about to give him the satisfaction of that. I sit down, feeling like I have passed some sort of test, and I wait for him to tell him what he wants me to do now.

"Did Mel show you where the storage room is? For the archived paper work?" Luke asks and I nod. "And did she show you the room next to it?"

"We didn't go inside, but she told me it was for photo-copying, shredding and scanning," I reply. "Oh, and for filing current paper work."

"Good," Luke says. "I want you to go into the storage room, which unfortunately has become a bit of a mess in recent years and go through all of the archived paper work. For tax reasons, we have to keep the last seven years' worth of paper work. The current year's stuff is either in the photo-copy room as you rightly pointed out, or it is still with its relevant department, so you need only worry about last year's files and then the five years previous to that. The paperwork for those times should all be organized properly and archived in some sort of sensible order. And anything older than that needs to be shredded. Do you have any questions?"

I am tempted to ask him why he thinks it's the best use of my time to do something like that when I'm a qualified web developer, but I don't. I know better than to say something like that and get fired on my first day. Louisa would love that one. I know I just have to suck it up and do the useless tasks to prove I am capable of following instructions and then I will get to do something more interesting. Or if not, at least I am being paid for it. If it was an unpaid internship, I would be much angrier than I actually am.

Just suck it up. Think of the wages and think of the reference I say a few times in my head like it's my new mantra. And maybe it will come to that.

"No," I reply. "It sounds straightforward enough."

"There's a staff meeting at four o'clock that I want you to attend. Other than that meeting, this archiving and shredding is your priority," Luke says. "Off you go."

I hate being dismissed like a naughty child, but yet again, I bite my tongue. I don't know why Luke is seemingly trying to get underneath my skin, but I don't think he usually acts like this judging by Mel's reaction to his rude words earlier. I guess his attitude and the shitty task he has given me to do is a kind of hazing. Well, if he wants to see what I'm made of, then I'll show him it'll take more than a bit of menial work and a bad attitude to break me.

I see it's going to be way more than a bit of menial work when I open the door to the storage room; it's going to be more like a year of menial work. Luke wasn't kidding when he said it had become a bit of a mess in here. Each wall of the room is lined with shelves and on those shelves are boxes of paper work, files and folders, with loose sheets spilling everywhere and from what I can see at a quick glance, nothing is labelled.

I spend a moment deciding how best to complete the task. I decide to tackle the biggest boxes first and use one of them to store the paper work from the years I need to keep and use another one of them to store the paper work for shredding.

Then every time the shredding box gets full, I will drag it next door and do the shredding and then come back and rinse and repeat until all the shredding is done. When everything is shredded that needs to be done, then I'll work on organizing the rest of the paperwork, the bits we need to keep, by sorting it by year and then by subject and getting it all filed away in some sort of order. Once I have a plan of attack worked out, I feel much better about tackling the task in front of me, although I still think it is going to be a long, difficult and tiring job. Maybe six months job rather than a year or two.

I shrug off any negativity I'm still feeling. I have to do the task whether I like it or not, so I might as well do it to the best of my ability and stop moaning in my head about it. That will only make is seem worse. I drag the first big box to the floor and then the second one, and then I sit down and take the lids off them and empty them both out. I begin scanning over the documents for dates and then sorting them into either the keep and or the shred box depending on what it is.

By the time lunch time comes around, I have my system nailed and I'm getting through the paperwork a lot quicker than I had expected to. While a lot of it is a mess, some of the boxes aren't as jumbled as others and are nice and easy to get through. I know I will work better on a full stomach than an empty one though, and I take a quick twenty-minute break for lunch where I run out to buy and eat a sandwich, use the ladies' room and then go back to work with a cup of coffee. The coffee here really is good.

I make sure to keep a watch on the time as I work, conscious of the fact that I have to be at the staff meeting at four o'clock and not wanting to forget about it or be late to it. At three forty five, I finish up my last shredding of the day and return the empty box back to the store room. I figure I probably have time to do a bit more sorting, but the last thing I want to do is to leave it too late and then not be able to find the meeting room or something stupid like that and be late for the meeting in front of everyone. And I have a feeling Luke will call me out on it if I am late in and he will likely do it in front of everyone.

I decide it's better to seem like I'm there too early than too late and so I walk along to the elevator. I decide for the sake of going down one floor, I'll take the stairs when I see that the elevator is currently on the first floor – it will likely be quicker. I go through the door marked 'stairs' and walk down to the floor below me. I walk along the corridor, looking into the rooms, hoping to find some clue as to where I'm meant to be.

I see a small room with people in it, but the room doesn't look big enough to hold ten people comfortably, let alone the entire staff and rather than risk disturbing people who might have nothing to do with the meeting, I keep going. Right at the end of the hallway, the floor opens out into a huge space. Rows of chairs have been laid out, all facing towards the front, and I figure this must be where I'm meant to be. Some of the chairs are already occupied, but a lot aren't yet. I glance at the seated people, and I choose to approach a woman sitting alone in the third row. She looks friendly enough.

"Hi," I say. "I'm new here. Is this where the staff meeting is being held?"

"Yes," the woman replies. "You're new you say?"

I nod, and the woman indicates with a hand for me to sit down next to her. Glad to have someone to talk to until the meeting starts, I sit down gratefully.

"I'm Tracy," she says. "I work in accounts."

"Louisa," I say. "I'm just an intern."

"How long have you been here?" Tracy asks.

"It's my first day," I tell her.

"How are you finding it?" she asks.

Again, I decide to err on the side of caution. Just because

she's nice and chatty doesn't mean she won't tell Luke the intern has been moaning about her work.

"I like it so far," I say. "Everyone I've met has been really nice to me."

"Most everyone here is nice," she says. "Like anywhere, there are a few people who are a bit standoffish, but for the most part, we all get along just fine. What department are you working in?"

"My field is web development, and I hope to end up working there, but at the moment, I'm doing a task for Luke," I say.

"Oh. You must be special," Tracy says with a laugh. "Luke normally doesn't really have anything to do with the interns."

I laugh along with her, but I am surprised to hear that. I'm nothing special. But then I remember he thinks I'm a board member's daughter. It makes sense he might take a special interest in me thinking that, but at the same time, it makes less sense that he would have me doing the crap he has me doing. I can't figure the man out and I decide to stop even trying.

More and more people are filing in now and the chairs are filling up fast. I spot Mel and Rachel coming in together and I spot Susan coming in with a younger man. Right at four o'clock, Luke appears, and the conversations tail off and everyone pays attention to him without him having to say a word.

He talks about figures and projections and ad campaigns and more. I must admit I kind of tune out. I try to stay engaged, but the stuff he's talking about doesn't affect me and I always find that my mind wanders if I'm not interested in what's being said.

I force myself to tune back in when I catch my attention drifting off. It's almost five o'clock and Luke is still talking. I can see a lot of the staff are starting to get a bit restless, knowing that the end of the working day is fast approaching. Even though I'm contracted to work from nine am to five pm like everyone else, I make sure I don't look like I'm eager to leave because I don't think that is the best impression to give on a first day anywhere, especially not for the person on the lowest rung of the ladder.

"And finally, we have a new member of staff joining us today. Louisa? Where are you? Stand up," Luke says.

I look around with everyone else. I want to see this new girl because it's good to know I'm not the only newbie, and it might be good to befriend the other new starter. No one stands up and Luke calls the name again. Tracy gently digs her elbow into my ribs.

"Stand up Louisa," she whispers.

I feel the blood rush to my face with embarrassment as I get to my feet. I am embarrassed because for a moment there, I genuinely forgot that I'm meant to be Louisa, but I'm confident that anyone who notices my obvious discomfort will think it's because I have to stand up in front of everyone. In fairness, I probably would have blushed at that anyway so they wouldn't be entirely wrong.

"Everyone, this is Louisa. Louisa, this is everyone," Luke says.

I do an awkward little wave while people shout out greetings and welcomes to me. Although it is embarrassing, it's also kind of nice because of the welcome I receive.

"Louisa is our newest intern," Luke explains. "Please make her feel welcome here."

The room starts to clap, and I feel my cheeks reddening once more. I don't know where to look so I look down at the ground, wanting it to open up and swallow me. Finally, the applause dies out.

"Welcome to Sold, Louisa," Luke says. "That's the meeting over. See you all tomorrow."

He walks back out of the meeting without another word, or a backward glance and I'm relieved that I am no longer the only person on their feet. I say goodbye to Tracy and hurry away. I go back up the stairs because I figure the elevator car will be packed full. I don't know what to do. Luke made it clear it is home time for everyone, but as an intern, am I expected to stay until I'm dismissed? Or until I finish my task? God, I hope that's not the case, I'll be here until midnight next Tuesday.

I come through the door at the top of the stairs, and I see Mel walking along the hallway in front of me. I call out to her, and she stops and turns around. She smiles at me and waits for me to catch up.

"How's your first day gone?" she says.

"It's flown by actually," I say, which is both true and a nice way to avoid having to answer the question based on my menial task. "I'm just wondering what happens now. Do I finish the task Luke has given me before I leave, or do I wait for him to come and dismiss me, or …?"

I tail off at the end, not sure what else to add. Mel shakes her head.

"No, you don't have to wait for permission to leave. As long as you've done your eight hours, you can leave generally speaking. Obviously, there might be times where there is urgent work needed and you will be expected to stay and work over if you are a part of that, but otherwise, you finish at five unless you're late in or told otherwise," Mel says.

"Thanks Mel," I reply.

"No worries," Mel says. We have reached our respective offices and Mel smiles at me. "Catch you tomorrow. Assuming you're coming back?"

"Oh, I'm coming back alright. See you tomorrow," I reply.

I go into my tiny office and retrieve my coat and my purse and then I make my way to the end of the corridor, and this time, I choose to wait for the elevator. The doors open finally, and I step in and turn to see Luke getting in behind me. I hit the ground floor button and look up at him.

"Ground floor?" I say and he nods his head.

"Who told you that you could leave for the day?" he says.

"Umm, Mel," I reply.

I don't want to get her in trouble, but it's true and I figure she is much less likely to catch a pile of shit than I am.

"Oh, right. That's ok then," he says, and he looks at me for a moment and then he smiles. "I was joking, Louisa."

I manage to fake a laugh that sounds reasonably normal, but I don't think he was joking. I think he just said that to save face when I said Mel said I should leave. I think if I hadn't have said that he would have had a go at me, maybe even demanded I stay over to finish the shredding and sorting.

He's definitely one to watch, this man, and he's easy enough on the eye that I'm more than willing to watch him.

# CHAPTER
## Six

**LUKE**

I don't know why, but as I'm sitting at my desk working on a report, Louisa pops into my head. I try to tell myself it's not because I fancy the ass off her, and it's certainly not because I'm intrigued by her, it's just because I'm wondering how far along she is with the task I gave her yesterday. Probably not very far. I would expect a motivated employee to take a few days to get through that lot, but a work shy one, God it could take weeks. The thing is though, despite Enrique's warning, Louisa seems anything but work shy to me at the moment. She must be a bloody good actress is all I can say, or else she's appearing motivated at first until she figures she's out from underneath my radar and then her true colors will show through.

I decide to go and see how far she has gotten and tell her she needs to hurry it up and stop wasting company time. I feel a bit harsh for doing it, but I promised Enrique that I would whip her into shape, and I'm hardly going to do that if I just believe she's actually working out ok and just ignore her, and if she doesn't leave here better than she was when she started, I won't have Enrique's favor when I need him to vote with me.

I save my work and close down the report and then I leave my office and head along to the storage room. I reach it and open the door. I don't know what I'm expecting exactly. A mess definitely. Maybe I will even catch Louisa sitting around messing about on her cell phone instead of working. The last thing I expect is what I actually see.

The mess is gone. A stack of empty boxes stands neatly in one corner and the rest of the paper work is boxed and all of the boxes are on the shelves. Louisa turns to see who has come in.

"I just need to finish up the labels and stick them on the boxes and then I'm done," she says. "I'm sorry it took a while, but it really was in quite a state."

"No, no, it's fine. You've done well here," I say. Spoiled brat or not, she has more than exceeded the expectations I would have had for someone I knew that would just come in and get on with the task, let alone for her, and there's no way I can berate her for this without making myself look like an idiot or a bully, neither of which are a good look. I think on my feet, and I know exactly what I can do to get her bratty side to come out. "When you've finished your labelling, come along to my office. I have another task for you."

Louisa nods her head.

"Ok," she says, "I won't be long", and she goes back to her labels.

I leave the storage room and close the door gently behind me. There's a board meeting this afternoon, and I need someone to go out and get some groceries and prepare snacks for the table, and also, to serve drinks throughout the meeting. I know Louisa will absolutely hate doing that from what Enrique has told me about her.

It's one thing being forced to do manual labor that you believe you're too good for behind closed doors, but being told she has to publicly wait on people is another matter entirely. That will get her spoiled side raging, and she will likely throw a bitch fit. And then when she does, I can start showing her how the real world works, and how in business, you are a nobody until you have proved yourself, with or without your father's name.

I go back to my office, planning on finishing up the report I was working on while I wait for Louisa. Once I get back into my office and sit down, it occurs to me that sending Louisa off to buy the groceries might backfire on me. She might spend completely over budget, or she might come back with inappropriate things, and it will be a reflection on me. Even though I'm not the one who will have made the mistake, I am the one who hands out the tasks, and someone is bound to question why I had an intern take charge of this rather than Donna who has actually been trained for the role and does it as part of her job, although the two are actually unrelated.

I think for a moment and then I start making a shopping list consisting of the kinds of things Donna usually serves – seafood, vegetable crudities and dips, charcuterie board ingredients, nice cakes and fresh cream eclairs, that kind of thing. I read back over the list, confident the spread will be of good enough quality and that the ingredients shouldn't cost more than one hundred dollars. I finally go back to the report and wait for Louisa to come to me. I wish I could make her come in other ways, but I push that thought firmly from my mind before it can take hold. There's no way I am getting myself involved with Enrique's daughter. No way at all.

# CHAPTER
*Seven*

## TIA

I stand at the head of the table in the conference room, the one where the board meeting is to be held. I look over the buffet I have put together and I smile. I'm quite pleased with it if I'm being honest. Luke gave me a shopping list and told me to get everything on it and not to go over one hundred dollars. It's clear Luke has never had to shop on a budget before, because I got everything on the list and a few extra things I thought would help to make the buffet look more upmarket, and I only spent seventy-three dollars and fifty-five cents. Luke seemed surprised when I gave him the receipt and change when I came back, but I thought he actually looked pleased too.

Now the buffet is done, all I have left to do is greet the board members as they arrive and take their drinks orders and serve them. That's definitely the easy part compared to the catering side, and I'm not worried at all about it.

I greet the first few arrivals and take their drinks orders. I make and serve the drinks without any mishaps, and I'm settling into the greeter role nicely when the next person appears, and I greet them and take their drink order too. I fall into a routine and the task gets done quickly and efficiently, even if I do say so myself.

Everyone is here now except for Luke and one board member, and I fully relax. I already know Luke's drink order, so I have literally one more order to do and I have already heard a few comments about the food looking nice.

I'm hanging around in the doorway to the meeting room waiting for the last board member to arrive. The meeting is due to start in five minutes and I know Luke won't turn up until the last minute so he can just dive straight into it if his performance in yesterday's meeting is anything to go by. I hear a woman's voice, and I realize she's speaking into a cell phone. I can't see her, but it's obvious because she speaks and then pauses. I figure she's the last board member and I continue to wait for her to appear.

"I told you I'd be late home tonight," the woman says. "I'm at Sold." Pause. "For the board meeting." Pause. "Yeah, no shit." Pause. "I'm sitting in for my dad, remember? Apparently, there's a few votes he thinks are too important for his vote not to be counted, so I'm just here to vote on his behalf."

It hits me then who the woman on the cell phone must be. Sophia Sanchez. Louisa's older sister. She is here to sit in for Enrique. That's it. That's my cover blown. It's not like I can just wander off and hide. Might that be better though? I can tell Luke I miscounted, and I thought everyone was here. No, don't give up so easily, I think to myself. Think. Come on. Think. He'll never buy that because even if I counted the board members wrong, I would know he wasn't here.

Sophia is saying her goodbyes on her call when the perfect idea comes to me and when I'm confident that she has ended the call, I step around the corner to meet her.

"Tia," she says, beaming when she sees me. "It's so good to see you."

Thankfully, she's alone, and I smile back at her.

"It's really good to see you too," I say. "But I need to ask you a favor. I know it probably won't make a difference, but I'm doing an internship here and I don't want Luke, my boss, to know I know Enrique in case he starts treating me differently. Can you just like pretend you don't know me in there?"

"Oh, sure if that's what you want," Sophia says. "If it will make you feel better, of course I will. But you don't have to worry. Between us, Luke is harder on Louisa because my dad told him she needs a bit of a reality check when it comes to work. I'm sure he wouldn't start being harder on you."

"I don't know," I say. "He gets us mixed up all the time anyway. It's got to the point where I answer to Louisa and Louisa answers to Tia. It's easier than to keep telling him."

"That's comical," Sophia laughs. "You two couldn't be any more different from each other to look at if you tried to be."

I laugh along with her and then I hear footsteps coming along the corridor.

"What can I get you to drink?" I say, hoping Sophia has heard the footsteps too and plays along.

"A black coffee, no sugar please," she says, and she tips me a wink and goes into the meeting room.

I relax a little bit. That's covered Sophia not calling me Tia in front of Luke and it's covered me if Luke calls me Lousia in front of Sophia. Now I just have to quickly speak to Luke. I hurry towards him.

"Can I have a quick word?" I say.

"Can't it wait?" he says, glancing at me with a look of irritation.

"Umm, not really," I say.

Luke sighs.

"It'll have to be mega quick. The meeting is starting," Luke says.

"It's just, I didn't realize Sophia was coming to the meeting today or I would have said something sooner," I say. "My family isn't big on playing on personal connections at work is all I wanted to tell you. What I mean is, Sophia will act like I'm just another intern rather than her sister. I just wanted to ask you not to make a big deal out of it or draw attention to who I am in there."

"No, I won't. I'm not in the habit of introducing the interns to the board members," Luke says. "Or quizzing the board members on why they aren't chatting to the interns either."

"I realize that. I just didn't want you to think it was weird that Sophia wasn't speaking to me," I say.

"I honestly don't care and likely wouldn't have noticed, but no, I won't make a big deal out of it. Now run along and get my coffee," he says.

I bite my lip and nod and then I hurry away to make his coffee and Sophia's coffee. This time, I'm not biting my lip to keep from snapping back at Luke. I am biting it to stop myself from smiling. Sophia told me something that has completely changed the way I see Luke's treatment of me now. He doesn't hate me or think I'm useless. He thinks I am Louisa, and it sounds like Louisa's father has basically told Luke she can be a bit lazy and spoiled – his words not mine, but I know what he means to an extent. Luke is just trying to impress Enrique by being mean to me and I can live with that a lot easier than I could live with it when I thought it was actually against me personally.

And over the course of my time here, I might just help Louisa's father to see her in a whole new light when Luke goes back to him after the internship is done and tells him that actually I'm not lazy or work shy or spoiled, because I am none of those things and I really want a good reference here so as much fun as it might be to act like Luke was expecting Louisa to act, I won't do it and risk my future career.

# CHAPTER
*Eight*

## LUKE

I go into the meeting room and greet the board members and then we get down to business. As I'm well aware of what is to be discussed, I find my mind wandering when the vice chairman of the board starts speaking, and it lands on Louisa. I find it so strange that her and her sister don't acknowledge each other at work. I mean I get that Louisa might not want to rub it in people's faces that her father is on the board, but it's not like everyone doesn't know her name and they can surely put the pieces together. A simple acknowledgement is nothing, and there aren't even any staff here to see any interaction between the two.

Still, as odd as I find it, someone else's family dynamic has nothing at all to do with me and I'm not about to make a big deal out of it as Louisa put it. I can't help but compare the two women in my mind either. Sophia is visibly Latina with lovely olive colored skin and brown hair and eyes, and Louisa couldn't be further from that.

But the differences between them are not just physical.

Sophia and Enrique are so similar, both outgoing, confident and head strong. Louisa on the other hand seems quieter and more reserved, less likely to rock the boat so to speak.

I wonder for a moment if maybe Louisa is adopted. It would explain her Swedish mom and her physical differences from the other members of the Sanchez family. But that doesn't explain her totally different personality. Of course there will be some differences from person to person, but if Louisa was raised in the same house as Sophia, I would expect there to be at least some common ground and there's nothing. Plus, surely, she would have said she was adopted when I commented on how different she is to her father, rather than say her mother is Swedish.

I tune back into the meeting in time to cast my vote on the issue at hand and then the vice chairman of the board moves onto the next bullet point and my mind wanders once more, and once more, it comes to land on Louisa.

I wonder why Louisa felt the need to ask me not to comment on her and Sophia not speaking to each other. I mean she must have known I wouldn't be introducing her around and that I wouldn't really expect her to be hanging around chatting to any board members. And even if I thought it was odd they didn't acknowledge each other, I'm hardly going to draw attention to it and potentially embarrass Sophia in front of the other board members. Louisa must have known that I wouldn't do it, so she must have felt really strongly about it to even bother to bring it up.

That's when it hits me. What if Louisa is Enrique's daughter with another woman. What if he has a whole second family. Maybe Louisa found out somehow and that's why she was so adamant that I do not draw attention to her and Sophia because Sophia perhaps doesn't even know Louisa exists.

It sounds crazy, like the plot of a far-fetched soap opera,

but at the same time, it also feels like it might be the only logical explanation for all the little things that are bugging me about this scenario. And if that's the case, is Louisa really spoiled, or does Enrique want me to be harder on her to remind her she's second best, and not a part of his main family?

I don't know if that's true or not, but Louisa has done nothing to imply she's lazy or spoiled here and I decide it's time I start being a little bit nicer to her unless she gives me an actual reason to be harsh to her. There is a fine line between preparing someone for the real world and just being a dick to them and potentially making them hate their work.

# CHAPTER
## *Nine*

**TIA**

I head into work on Wednesday morning wondering what task I will be given today. Maybe it will be cleaning the toilets or emptying the trash bins. If Luke thinks pulling stunts like that will scare me away, he really doesn't know a thing about me. I am not scared of hard work or getting my hands dirty. Of course, I would love to do something related to what I'm actually qualified to do, but I don't think the jobs I'm being given are beneath me and I will just get on and do them. When it comes down to it, I want a reference and it's not going to say on there what specific tasks I was doing, so it doesn't matter to me what I do really. If Luke thinks the best use of my time is doing menial work, then that's his bad call not mine, especially as he is the one paying me.

I've barely gotten my coat off when Mel is behind me telling me that Luke wants to see me in his office. I thank her and head to the office. I'm a little bit nervous, but it's not because I'm afraid of Luke or what he might be about to say, it's because I know I am about to confronted with his hand-some face and his lush body and I'm worried I will say or do something to give away that I fancy the ass off him. It doesn't matter that I'm not going to act on it, just having Luke know I have this crush on him would still be as embarrassing as hell and definitely something I can do without.

I go the Luke's office and go in when he shouts for me to enter. I sit down in the chair opposite his when he gestures towards it. I was right. He is looking as good as ever and I have to force myself to focus on his words rather than on the way his lips draw my attention when they move to talk, or how I think they would feel on my body, sucking my nipple, moving lower, working my clit and drinking from my pussy.

"Louisa? Are you ok? You're looking a bit flushed," Luke says and of course that does nothing to rectify the situation, and I feel myself flushing even darker.

"Yes, I'm fine," I manage to say. "I'm just a bit hot, that's all."

I fan my face with my hand to demonstrate, you know, in case he doesn't know what being a bit hot means. Luke jumps up and goes and opens a window. A light breeze blows in.

"Is that better?" he asks.

I nod. It's a really nice breeze actually and although I'm not really hot enough to be flushed, I was on the hot side, and I appreciate the fresh air blowing in.

"How do you feel like your first two days have gone?" Luke asks me, sitting back down.

"Ok," I say. "I feel like I'm settling in, and everyone is really nice and welcoming. It would be nice to get the chance to do something IT related though."

I hadn't planned to say that last part, but I'm glad that I did. I don't think it was rude or anything like that and even if it doesn't happen, at least Luke knows I'm keen to get my teeth into something useful.

"You know what makes a good employee?" Luke says. I figure it's a rhetorical question and so I don't even try to answer. It seems I made the right assumption when Luke goes on. "Doing whatever task is given to them that benefits the company in some way. And you know what makes a good intern? Doing whatever task is given to them that benefits the company in some way without moaning about doing it."

"I was hardly moaning. I was just answering your question. I have done everything you've asked of me without moaning so much as once," I fire back, slightly annoyed now.

"That's true I suppose," Luke relents. "And I think maybe you'll find this next task to be unrelated to IT and therefore not suited to you, but I am going to have you do it anyway."

"I figured," I say and is that the hint of a smile I actually see on Luke's face. No, it can't be. It must be wind.

"Rachel, my receptionist is on leave until Monday. You will be filling in for her. You'll be answering and directing calls – any that ask for me personally, find out who it is. If it seems important, forward it to Mel. If not, just tell them I'm unavailable. In between calls, you will be filing and doing whatever Mel asks you to do. Basically, the tasks she doesn't want to do. Do you think you can manage that?" Luke says.

"As hard as it sounds, I'm sure I can soldier through," I say sarcastically.

If Luke notices my sarcasm, he doesn't let on.

"Glad to hear it," Luke says. "Did Mel explain to you about your timesheet?"

I nod, surprised by the sudden jump in subjects.

"What did she say?" Luke asks.

"To record my start and finish times every day and email my time sheet to payroll on Friday," I say.

"That's standard procedure, but I would like you to send

your time sheet to me to approve and I will forward it on for you," Luke says.

"Do you think I'm going to try and claim extra hours?" I ask, shocked that he would think such a thing.

"Not at all," Luke says. "I don't think that for a second."

He doesn't explain any further and I feel like if I press him for a reason, he's just going to shut me down, so I don't say anything else. Even if he does think I would try to claim extra hours, he will soon see that he is wrong. I have nothing to hide, and I would never try to rob from a company who took a chance on me, even if they do think I'm someone else.

I decide then that Luke probably doesn't think I would falsify my time sheet. After all, he thinks I'm the daughter of one of the major shareholders. Aside from that making me pretty rich in my own right if it were really the case, it would also mean that stealing time from the company would be like stealing from my own father, something he can't possibly think I would do.

I stand up abruptly.

"Well, I'd best get to work," I say.

"Who said we were done here?" Luke asks.

I really thought we were, but the truth is, no one said it. I think for a moment and decide to beat Luke at his own game.

"Perhaps if you have anything further to say to me, you could come to my office, because I would hate to waste so much as a minute of company time," I say sweetly but Luke knows as well as I do that I am being massively sarcastic, and this time, he doesn't let it go.

"Sit down this instant," Luke shouts.

I do as he says, swallowing hard. I've gone too far, and I don't really blame him for being angry with me.

"What on earth has gotten into you Louisa?" Luke demands when I've sat back down in front of him once more. "Your attitude today is terrible."

I try to think of something believable, and in the end, I settle for a crumb of truth.

"I thought I would be who you think I am," I say.

"Huh?" Luke says. "What does that even mean?"

"Well let's just say someone might have let it slip about my father telling you I am lazy and spoiled and to be harder on me. It makes no difference how well I perform on any task you give me you're never going to trust me with anything useful," I say.

"Ah. You heard about that," Luke says, and he has the decency to look a bit embarrassed. "Full disclosure. You're right about what your dad said to me. Truthfully though I'm not finding anything to back up what he said. Prove yourself to me over these next few days and I will do the same to you. I will treat you like any other staff member, and we will see where we go from here once Rachel is back."

"Deal," I say. I grin at him. "I might even still make you a coffee when I have one."

"Oh yes, that will never stop being a thing," Luke says, returning my grin, and for the first time, I get a flash of what I think might be the real Luke instead of the one Louisa's father asked him to be. "That's all for now. If you need any help with the telephone system or anything, Mel is just across from you, and she will help you."

"I think I'll be ok, but thank you," I say and this time when I get up, Luke doesn't yell for me to sit back down.

I go back to my office and see that my desk phone has been pushed over so that another phone can take its place. This one is more of a switch board, but although it looks kind of intimidating, I'm sure I'll be fine on it. On one of my jobs, I operated a switch board much more complicated than this one. That's how I was able to confidently tell Luke I thought I would be ok.

As I sit waiting for my first call, email, or piece of filing to come in, I start thinking about how much better I felt when I told Luke I knew why he was treating me poorly and how nice it was just to have that secret out in the open and have him lose the attitude he's so far had towards me. It makes me want to tell him the full truth, but I am far from ready for that. I really think he will flip his lid if he finds out Louisa and I tricked him like that and I can almost guarantee I will be fired. It will be bye bye reference and possibly bye bye bestie when Louisa finds out I blabbed.

I'm just going to leave well enough alone there. I know that means I can never date Luke because the whole relationship would be based on a lie, but if I told him the truth, I could still never date him because he would hate me. At least this way I get to see him and be around him. The most annoying thing is, despite how gorgeous he is and how he looks like he could have any woman he wants, I get the impression he likes me too. Even though he's been a bit of a dick to me, I have caught him watching me when he didn't know I was looking and there's just something in his body language that tells me he fancies me as much as I fancy him. But none of that matters though. I need to stop thinking about Luke and start thinking about my job.

As though on cue, the telephone rings and I pick it up.

"Thank you for calling Sold. How can I help you?" I say.

The caller has a question about one of Sold's policies and rather than bothering Mel with it, I look up the information and answer the caller's question. I'm quite proud of myself when I end the call. For the next half an hour, the telephone rings constantly and I find my in tray filling up too. Even though all this still isn't what I really want to be doing, I am enjoying being kept busy and I think I'm coping quite well with everything over all. Of the seven calls I have taken so far, I had to transfer one to Mel because they wanted to speak to Luke about a supply issue which seemed important, I have told two callers Luke isn't available and left it at that, and the others, I have helped myself. Another call comes in now and I clear my throat and answer it.

"Thank you for calling Sold. How can I help you?" I say.

"Put me through to Luke Jackson please," the caller says.

"May I ask what it is regarding?" I ask.

"Board business. Now hurry up. The rates for calling from Europe are damned expensive you know," he says.

I cringe when I realize my caller is Enrique. Thank goodness he didn't seem to recognize my voice any more than I recognized his. The joys of a bad line.

"Right away, Sir," I say, and I put Enrique on hold while I dial through to Luke's office. He answers and I tell him I have Enrique on the line for him and put him through.

I haven't even replaced the receiver when Mel is standing in the doorway of my office.

"What the hell Louisa?" she demands. "You never put calls through to Luke without going through me."

"It … It was my father. He was moaning about the cost of the call, and I didn't want him to take it out on you if I transferred him to you instead of Luke," I stutter.

"Ok," Mel says, calmer now. "That's ok. Luke will always take a board member's call if he's available. It didn't even occur to me that it might be Enrique. Considering he's your dad, you didn't exactly speak warmly to him."

"I used the same professional tone I would with any board member. At work, that's all he is. It would be unprofessional to treat him like my dad while I'm at work," I say.

Mel considers this for a moment and makes a "mm" sound that could mean anything.

"Well, keep up the good work," she says, which is very different from the lecture this encounter started off with me getting.

I smile and nod that I will and then I take the top sheet

from my in tray and read through it to work out where I should file it. The current year's files are in the photocopying room and I'm confident I can do some filing in between calls and that if I leave the door to the photocopying room open while I'm in there filing, I will hear the phone ringing and it's only a few doors down so I can easily come back.

I decide where the paper belongs, and I stand up and edge around my desk. A shadow falls over me as I get ready to leave the office. I glance up and Luke is in my doorway.

"Is everything ok?" I ask.

Am I going to be in trouble for putting that call through, despite what Mel said?

"Yes," Luke says. "Your father wants to talk to you. He's still on the line."

Fuck. What do I do now? If I take this call, the ruse is up. I think on my feet.

"Tell him I'll call him on my break please," I say.

Luke opens his mouth, no doubt to argue with me, and I push past him and run to the ladies' room. The one place he can't follow me. I know he's going to be angry, but it's better than the alternative.

I pull my cell phone out of my jacket pocket as I sit on the closed lid of a toilet, and quickly text Louisa telling her she needs to call her dad and why. She texts back saying she will do it in ten minutes. That's the main problem dodged. Now I just have to face Luke and try to come up with something convincing to explain my rudeness. At least this time he's going to be pissed off with something I actually did, not some imagined crime Louisa's dad reported. I'm not sure if that's better or worse.

# CHAPTER
*Ten*

## LUKE

I stand for a moment, my mouth hanging open in shock as Louisa runs down the hallway away from me after rudely refusing to take her father's call, and then almost knocking me over as she pushed past me to leave her office.

"What the fuck was that?" Mel says from behind me, and I turn around to face her. She's standing in the doorway of her own office opposite the entry to Louisa's.

"You saw that too then?" I say. "Honestly, I was starting to think I imagined it."

"No, I saw it," Mel says. "She ran out of there like the building was on fire and you'd told her she couldn't leave."

I remember I have Enrique still on the line and I turn to go back to my office.

"When she comes back, tell her I want to see her," I tell Mel who nods her head and retreats back to her desk, where she can still see the entrance to Louisa's office.

I thought Louisa and I had made a bit of a break through when she confessed that she knew her father had asked me to be hard on her, but maybe not. Maybe now her true colors are showing. That doesn't feel right though. I feel like the hard working Louisa is the real one, and this rude side of her is some sort of an act. But now I know that she knows about what her father said, why would she put on an act that she's rude?

I shake my head. I don't think I'll ever figure this one out. I go back to my office and lift my receiver again.

"Enrique? Louisa isn't at her desk. I've left her a note to call you," I say.

"Damned girl, no doubt she's skiving off somewhere," Enrique says, and he hangs up the call before I can tell him that actually she doesn't seem like the type to do that at all. Maybe that's what that was all about. She hadn't had a chance to mentally prepare herself for the bashing her father was about to give her.

I don't know why I suddenly feel the need to defend her after her little outburst back there, but I do. I really don't like this affect she has on me. It feels like trouble waiting to happen.

I put Louisa out of my mind and focus on my own work until a timid knock sounds and I figure it's her. And if she's here in the flesh it's ok for her to be on my mind, because it would be weird for her not to be, so for the time she's here, I can at least stop trying to force myself not to think about her. I call for her to come in and the office door opens, and a very sheepish looking Louisa comes in.

"Close the door and sit down," I say.

Louisa does as I say and once she's seated, I raise an eyebrow.

"Well?" I say.

"Umm Mel said you wanted to see me," Louisa says.

"Playing dumb isn't helping your case here," I say. "Do you have any idea how embarrassing it was having to come back to Enrique and tell him you weren't where I thought you were?"

"I … I'm sorry," Louisa says. "I just don't want to mix my personal life with my professional life."

"I get that," I say. "And I respect it, but when I personally tell you to take a call, you do as I say. Ok?"

She nods her head.

"And an explanation for why you practically mowed me down to get out of the office instead of us having this conversation at the time would be nice," I add.

She doesn't say anything for a moment and then she blushes – she's so fucking sexy when she does that; it makes me think of how she would look if I made her come – and rubs her hands across her stomach.

"I had to use the bathroom," she says.

I almost ask her why it couldn't have waited a moment, but she's clearly embarrassed to be discussing this with me and I have no interest in discussing her toilet habits.

"Next time, a simple 'excuse me' would be nice," I say instead of pressing the issue.

"Of course, I'm sorry," Louisa says.

"Ok. Go back to work. And don't ever embarrass me like that again, do you understand?" I say.

She nods her head and practically runs from my office. I look at the closed door for a moment, imagining her scurrying away. It's almost like she was afraid to speak to Enrique on the phone. I can't help but wonder what the hell is going on there, but their family drama isn't my family drama. It's not like Louisa lives with Enrique so even if she is afraid of him, it's not like she's being abused at home or anything where I would feel the need to get involved.

No, she's a bit of a strange one, but I don't think it's any sort of abuse that's causing it, and I definitely don't think I should poke my nose in here. It's probably just what she said

– that she didn't want to seem unprofessional by taking a personal call at work. And maybe she felt nervous because I was blocking her path or something and she panicked and shoved out to stop herself from having a panic attack. Or maybe she really did have a stomach issue, and it was just awful timing.

That woman leaves a trail of questions whenever I speak to her, but there are two things I know for certain. One, Enrique is wrong about her work ethic, and two, I need to put some distance between us before I cross a line and tell her how I feel about her. It wouldn't be so bad if it was a one way street. I would just move on with my life. But I know Louisa likes me too. She tries very hard not to flirt with me, but I can't help but notice the subtle hair pulling, or the nibbling on her lower lip when she listens to me. I don't even think she knows she's doing it, but it tells me she wants me as much as I want her.

Why on earth does her father have to be my most influential board member. That's just my fucking luck.

# CHAPTER
## Eleven

**TIA**

I t's Friday lunch time, and as I sit in the breakroom with a cheese pasta salad, I think back over the last few days. I have quite enjoyed the receptionist work, and I would be quite happy to continue on with that if it came to it, but I know Rachel, the actual receptionist, is back from her leave on Monday and I won't be doing her job while she's here obviously. I really hope I don't have to go back to doing the shit jobs like sorting out the archiving and doing the catering. I get that they are tasks that need to be done, but I want to take on something bigger, something a bit more meaningful. Luke keeps saying I have to prove myself, but how can I prove myself if he isn't giving me anything to do that I can use to show him my skills. Anyone can shred old papers or put prawns on a plate. I want to show him I know my stuff when it comes to web development.

I decide that after lunch, I'm going to go and talk to him and find out what he has planned for me, and if it sounds like make work, I'm going to request something a bit more challenging. The worst that can happen is he says no, and I'm still stuck with the shitty jobs, but hopefully he will see me taking some initiative and give me a chance. Maybe that's what he's waiting for. Maybe that's what he means by me proving myself. And if it isn't, well at least I will know I tried.

I finish the last forkful of my pasta salad and stand up. I put the container in the trash can and wash and dry my fork. I put it away and I stand for a moment leaning against the counter, just staring off into space. It seems that now it has come to be time to go and talk to Luke, some of my moxie has gone away.

I force myself away from the counter I'm leaning against, and I walk towards the break room door and into the hallway. I head to Luke's office before I can change my mind altogether. I remind myself once more that really, the worst thing that can happen here is Luke saying no to my request and that won't make me any worse off than I am now.

I reach the door to Luke's office, and I knock on it. I wait until I hear him shout for me to come in and I open the door and see Luke sitting in his normal seat. This time though, he isn't alone. A member of staff I vaguely recognize but don't really know is sitting opposite him.

"Oh, I'm so sorry, I didn't know you had someone in with you. I'll come back later," I say and start to back out and pull the door closed.

I know I won't build up the courage for this again today and I wonder whether that's a good thing or a bad thing. Have I saved myself from being told no and getting embarrassed about it, or have I gotten in my own way and ruined the chance of getting a better opportunity? I guess I will never know. Except … The employee stands up and smiles at me.

"It's ok, we were done here anyway," he says.

"Yes, come on in Louisa," Luke echoes and I step

awkwardly inside while they make a few more comments to each other.

The man smiles at me on his way out and I return the smile. Once he has gone, Luke indicates the chair opposite him. I sit down and find it's still warm from the previous occupant. Luke smiles at me.

"What can I do for you Louisa?" he asks.

You could swipe the desk clear, throw me on it and fuck me to within an inch of my life I think to myself.

"I wanted to talk to you about next week," I say instead. Luke nods his head and waits for me to go on. "Rachel is back so obviously I won't be doing her job anymore, and I wanted to ask you to give me a chance with something a bit more challenging. I will obviously do whatever you need me to do, and I will do so without complaint, but I feel like I'm letting myself down if I don't at least ask for an opportunity to prove to you that I am good at what I do."

Luke doesn't answer me immediately, but he doesn't look angry either so I guess it's not as bad as it could be.

"You have shown that you will throw yourself into any task given to you, and I have no doubt that you are very capable," Luke says finally. "I will think about it and let you know what you will be doing when I've decided what your next task will be."

"Thank you," I say.

I nod to Luke then I get up and leave his office. What he said to me wasn't exactly the answer I had hoped for – an instant yes – but it was much better than what I had dreaded – an instant no. And it is still possible that Luke is going to trust me with something challenging. And I genuinely believe he will think about it, because he had no reason to lie to me. If he had already decided what I would be doing and it was something else menial and he wasn't willing to at least consider changing his mind about it, I think he would have just said so. He doesn't seem to be too worried about keeping me happy and I don't think he'd start now.

I head back to my desk, upping my pace when the telephone starts to ring. As much as I have settled into this role, I won't miss the sound of that damned telephone ringing every few seconds.

# CHAPTER
## *Twelve*

## LUKE

I have spent the afternoon debating Louisa's request for a more challenging role next week. In truth, I would have handed her over to the web development team on the first day of her internship and let the team leader there assess her capabilities and assign her work if she had been any normal intern. But because of Enrique's warnings, I haven't done that; instead, I have kept her with me so I could keep an eye on her. She hasn't shown any of the negative qualities Enrique had told me to expect, and for that, I think she does deserve a chance at going and doing something IT related. But at the same time, I'm left wondering if she is just acting like she's a hard worker until I drop my guard a little bit and send her somewhere where I won't be her direct line supervisor.

I really am not sure what to do for the best, and it doesn't help that anytime I come down more on the side of giving her the chance she has asked for – a move I greatly respect for the record – and probably deserves, I then begin considering the fact I won't get to see much, if anything, of her. I know deep down that I can't let myself decide Louisa's fate based on that though. It isn't right for the company, for Louisa, or for Enrique's pocket. But it's still not easy. Every time I think I know what I'm going to do, I consider something I hadn't thought of. Finally, it gets to the point where I'm annoying myself going back and forth on this. I have never been indecisive like this, especially not over what really should be a simple decision. In that moment, I decide on my best course of action.

I decide to have Mel call Karl to come to my office so I can discuss it with him. If I am going to let Louisa loose on a real project, it will be something in the web development area because she said that was where her expertise lay, and I trust her to know her own abilities. Karl is the supervisor in charge of that team, and I want to know what he thinks about taking Louisa over there and having her lend a hand, with the obvious caveat that if she stirs up trouble or refuses to do her work, to send her straight back to me.

I pick up my desk phone receiver and call through to Mel's office.

"What's up?" she says in the way of greeting. She obviously knows it's an internal call or I'm sure she wouldn't make that her greeting.

"It's Luke," I say. "Can you find Karl from web development and have him come to my office please?"

"Sure," Mel says. "Anything else?"

"I'd love a coffee," I tell her.

"Should I ask Louisa to make it?" Mel asks, confused because I told her at the start of this thing to always have Louisa make the coffee.

"No," I say. "I'd actually like you to make it and make her one too while you're at it. She drinks caramel macchiato."

"OK," Mel says.

The part about the coffee is just a last minute thing that came to me while I was on the call to Mel. I want Louisa to know that I do value her both as an employee and as a person, even if it turns out that now isn't the right time for her to take on more complicated jobs. I think she'll like the fact that I remembered her coffee order. I tell myself I don't care about shit like that, but the truth is, I do care. And I want her to be happy about it.

When there's a knock on my door after a few minutes have gone by, instead of calling come in I get up and open the door. I want to be able to hear Louisa's reaction when she gets her drink, and if Mel asks why I'm opening the door, I'll tell her I just figured I'd help her because her hands are full. I'm greeted by Mel with three steaming mugs of coffee. I smile at her and take mine from her.

"Thanks," I say.

I watch her walk to her office. She presumably off loads her coffee because she comes back out after a few seconds with only one cup in her hand. She approaches Louisa's door and smiles.

"I brought you a cup of coffee," she says.

"Oh. Thank you," I hear Louisa say. "But isn't making the coffee my job?"

"As an intern I guess so, but you're acting as Rachel at the moment and while she does make the majority of the drinks, I sometimes make them."

"Luke said I had to make his coffee for the foreseeable future," Louisa says. "I hope he isn't angry about this, thinking I'm trying to get out of making it."

Mel shakes her head.

"He won't. In fact, it was him who told me your coffee order," Mel says.

I can imagine the smile on Louisa's face as she says 'oh ok' back to Mel. Mel goes back to her own office, and I go back into mine and close the door. I think Louisa did indeed appreciate my gesture. I tell myself I don't much care one way or the other, but I know it's a lie because of course I do care, and I'm pleased that she is happy.

Not long later, Karl comes to my office. After I tell him to sit down and we exchange a few pleasantries, I get right down to business.

"Work is beginning on the new app on Monday. Correct?" I say.

Karl nods his head.

"Yes," he says. "We have done all of the brainstorming, and we already know how we want it to look, what it will be able to do, how the interface is laid out for consumers. It's just a matter of putting it all together."

"Just," I say, laughing at Karl's nonchalance. "That's like a three week job."

"It'll be closer to five weeks with Diane missing," Karl says.

"That's actually why I called you up here," I say. "I have an intern who is wanting something more challenging to do and her speciality is web development. Do you think you could find a use for her, or will she just get under your feet? Be honest because I don't want anything derailing this or slowing it down further."

"I'm sure I could find work for her. And I'm not just saying that. Being short staffed is really making this too slow and at the minute, I don't think we will meet the deadline," Karl says. "An extra pair of hands might just turn things around for us."

"In the interest of full disclosure, and this goes no further than between us two, the intern in question is Enrique Sanchez's daughter. He's on our board of directors and he asked me to take his daughter, Louisa, on as an intern as a favor to him as he finds her lazy and uncooperative. I have to say I haven't seen that side of her. She has always been atten- tive and gets on with any work she is given. The task I gave her on Monday, realistically, I would have expected it to take a good few days and she had it finished by Tuesday morning. But if it turns out she's just putting on a show for me as her boss, I want you to know you have every right to give her an ass kicking, and if that doesn't work and she's not pulling her weight, feel free to let me know and I'll pull her straight off the project," I say.

"Got it," Karl says. "So, I'll be getting her on Monday then?"

I nod.

"Unless a different day is better for you?" I say.

"No, Monday is ideal because I can brief the whole team, her included, on what we're going to be starting," Karl says. "It means everyone knows the same information and I don't have to go over it twice."

"That's great. Thank you, Karl. And don't forget, if she becomes a problem, I want to know about it," I reiterate.

Karl nods his agreement and then he leaves my office, and I pick up my phone again and call along to Mel. She answers the call.

"Mel, it's Luke. Can you tell Louisa I want to see her please. It's not urgent, her work is more of a priority. She can pop in any time before she leaves for the day and it will be fine," I say.

"No problem," Mel says and cuts me off.

I roll my eyes and smile to myself. It's a good job Mel is the best personal assistant I've ever had and that she doesn't do shit like that with potential advertisers, just with me. A few hours pass and then Louisa is back in my office and sitting down, having informed me that Mel said I wanted to see her.

"On Monday, the web development team is starting a new

project. They will be working on a new app," I say. "They are a team member down and it's going to make things hard for them. I realize I could replace Diane who has left, but these posts require a special sort of person, and I hate to just take the first person who comes along because it often makes things harder for the rest of the team than just being short staffed would. I would like to be able to take the time to find someone for the role who will fit in with the team and be a good match."

Louisa nods her head.

"That makes sense," she says. "Do you want me to go on Monster and other sites like that and find potential candidates for you?"

"Would you consider that a more suitable role for someone with your degree than say, working the reception desk?" I ask.

"Not really," Louisa admits. "But as you said, a good intern does whatever they are asked to do without moaning."

I smile and she smiles back.

"God, I can be a right dick, can't I?" I say.

She looks shocked for a moment and then she laughs and nods her head.

"A bit," she says.

When the laughter has died down, I get to the point.

"I don't want you messing around with resumes and that stuff. That's what HR is for. Well amongst other things. No, I have spoken to Karl, the supervisor in that department, and we have decided to give you a chance on the team," I say.

Louisa's jaw drops and for a moment, she just sits there, frozen. She blinks and closes her mouth.

"Are you being serious?" she says.

"Deadly serious," I tell her.

She makes a squeaking sound and throws her head back and laughs. She sits back up and tries to stop the laughter. She is mostly successful, but she can't quite stop her smile. I smile back at her.

"I take it that means you're happy then?" I say and she nods her head.

"Yes. More than I can explain. Thank you so much. I won't let you down, I promise," she says.

"Please don't," I say. "Because I have made it clear to Karl that he is your boss for the duration of your time on his team and if you drag your feet or don't perform, he's not going to put up with it."

"I wouldn't expect him to," Louisa says. "So, on Monay do I come up here first or just go straight to the web development team?"

"You can go straight to the team. Karl is expecting you," I say.

"Perfect. Thank you again," Louisa says on her way out.

She closes the door behind herself, and I smile. I can tell by her reaction how happy and proud of herself she is, and I love that for her, I really do. And I tell myself that I am not in the least bit bothered that I probably won't see her again for the duration of her internship unless she does let me down, and I genuinely don't think she will do that.

# CHAPTER
## Thirteen

**TIA**

I walk back to my tiny office like I'm floating on air. If it wasn't for the fact that I just know someone would appear from somewhere and catch me, I would be doing a happy dance right about now. As it is, I can't keep the smile off my face as I squeeze around my desk and tell myself I won't have to do that anymore after today. I can't believe Luke is giving me this chance. I know I asked him to consider something more challenging, but even in my wildest dreams, where I thought he might agree to it, I didn't think he would give me an opportunity like this. I am so excited, and I almost wish it was Monday now. It's strange to think that I will be wishing the weekend away so I can get back to work rather than it being the other way around.

I take my cell phone out of my pocket and send both Louisa and Justin text messages with my news. Louisa texts back instantly. She sends a heart emoji and says congratulations, but then she also says that she has to go out of state this weekend, because her and her new boyfriend have a trip planned already, but that we'll do something to celebrate when she's back. I reply telling her to have a good time, even though I am secretly a bit gutted that I won't be able to celebrate with her over the weekend.

Justin's reply comes in just as I'm about to put my cell phone back away. He too congratulates me, and he invites me for drinks tonight to celebrate. I hesitate for a moment before I reply to him. I want to say yes, but I keep thinking about what Louisa said about him wanting to get back with me. I don't think it's true though and I ignore her warning voice in my head and text Justin back saying I'd love to. I tell him to meet me at Ray's, a bar not far from my apartment, at seven. That will give me time to finish work, get home, eat and change. His reply comes in quickly and it's simply a thumbs up emoji.

I put my cell phone back away and concentrate on getting the last of the filing and typing done. I don't want to make Luke regret his choice before Monday even comes around by starting to slack off now.

I finished work pretty much on time and went home. I put a pizza in the oven and while it was cooking, I jumped in the shower and washed and dried my hair. I paused in my getting ready routine to eat, and then put some fresh makeup on and got dressed in a pink body con dress that sits just above my knee along with silver heels, purse and jewelery. I walked to the bar and made it in plenty of time although Justin was still there before me. He stood up when he saw me coming and after greeting me, he went to the bar without asking what I wanted and came back with an expensive bottle of champagne in an ice bucket and two flutes. I objected to the amount he must have spent on the bottle, but he insisted he wanted to treat me because I deserved it, and I didn't want to make a scene, so I accepted the drink graciously.

That bottle is gone now and we're onto our second one. I'm more than a little bit tipsy, but I'm far from being really drunk. I'm at that nice level of almost drunk where I feel all warm and cosy inside. Justin has just finished telling me about how he is almost finished renovating a house he bought here on the cheap and how he is debating between staying living there or selling it, at a profit and doing the same thing on another house.

"I've just realized something," Justin says, reaching for the champagne bottle and topping both of our glasses up. "I asked you out tonight to celebrate your good news and all I've done is go on and on about the house."

"It's ok," I said. "I asked you about it."

"And now I'm asking you about your news. Tell me all about your job," he says.

"Well so far, I haven't really done anything worth reporting. This first week has been about me proving that I am not work shy or spoiled, and now I think I've done that, and that's why I'm getting a chance to join the web development team on Monday," I say.

"That's perfect for you," Justin says, and I nod.

"I know. I can't wait to get started," I tell him.

"I get that as an intern you might have to start at the bottom, but did your boss seriously tell you he wanted to make sure you weren't work shy and spoiled? That seems a bit rude and rather presumptuous don't you think?" Justin says.

"He didn't actually say that. I said that's what I figured he was doing, and he agreed. I don't think he would have said anything if I hadn't said it first. And honestly, I don't think he does that to every intern. I think it's just because of what my dad said to him," I say.

Justin frowns for a moment and looks at me.

"What?" I say.

"You're in touch with your dad?" he asks. "Why didn't you tell me that sooner?"

I shake my head.

"No. Of course I'm not in touch with my dad. If I was, I would have told you sooner, but I'm most definitely not. What even made you think that?" I say, confused.

"You just said you thought your boss was treating you worse than other interns because of what your dad said to him," Justin points out.

Did I say that? No, I wouldn't have done. But why the hell would he make that up? I realize what I've done, and I giggle. I think the champagne has gone to my head a little bit more than I first thought.

"I meant Louisa's dad," I say.

"Why would Louisa's dad say those things about you?" Justin says. "I assume you asked him for a reference. And he did that to you?"

"No, nothing like that," I say.

"Then what is it like?" Justin asks.

I know I've said too much, but I also feel like I have to explain it all now or have Justin think I've gone a bit mental. It won't hurt anything. It's not like he knows Luke or Enrique or works in the same field or anything. And besides, he is my friend. Even if he did know them, he wouldn't get me into trouble with with them.

"You can't tell anyone I've told you this," I say. "Promise."

"Scout's honor," Justin says, doing a salute.

"Where you even in the scouts?" I say.

"Well, no, but you get the sentiment. I promise I won't say anything to anyone about what you're going to tell me," he says.

That will have to do.

"So, Louisa's dad is on the board of directors at the company I am interning at. He got the internship for Louisa because she needs so much experience as a condition of a job offer she has. She didn't want to do the internship, and I was desperate for a job in my field. This is a paid internship, and they are so rare you wouldn't believe it. So, we decided I would do the internship. We will make a copy of the reference, and both use it. I get paid and Louisa gets her dad off her case, and we all win," I say. "So, yeah, I just have to pretend I'm Louisa. When her dad told Luke I'm lazy and spoiled he thought he was talking about Louisa."

Justin is quiet for a moment and then he shakes his head.

"That bloody girl will get you shot one of these days and you'll just blindly follow her to the end of the gun barrel," he says.

It's not the reaction I'm expecting at all. I thought he might be a bit shocked, but honestly, I thought he would laugh.

"What's that supposed to mean?" I say.

"Oh, come on Tia. Don't tell me you don't see that she's using you," he says. "You do the work, and she gets a reference."

"True. But I also get a reference, and I would never have gotten an opportunity like this without Louisa. It was getting to the point where I was considering taking on a full time unpaid internship and then waiting on tables or tending bar on an evening and weekend just to make my rent. Louisa saved me from that fate, and I am grateful to her for that, whether you like her or not," I say.

"Ok, I'm sorry," Justin says, holding his hands up in mock surrender. "I didn't know it had gotten that bad for you. And I don't not like Louisa. I just think she has too much influence over you."

"Why? Because she presented an idea that I agreed to because it benefited me too?" I say.

"Not just that. You moved to Chicago because she wanted you to," he points out.

"I moved to Chicago because the thought of staying alone in New York was killing me, and when I finally confessed how I felt to Louisa, she told me to come here so I would never have to be alone," I say.

"Ok. Again, I didn't know that" Justin says. "But there's still the major thing." He looks down into his lap for a moment. "She is still the one who split us up." He looks up again and I shake my head gently.

"Don't do this," I say.

"I'm not doing anything. I'm not saying the breakup wasn't for the best, because we both know it was. I'm just saying that Louisa kind of pushed you into ending things before you and I really saw the truth," he says.

"She didn't push me. She just voiced an opinion that she didn't think we were good together and that I no longer seemed happy. She was right on both counts, but it took someone from the outside looking in to see it clearly like that," I say.

"Ok, you win. Louisa is a great friend and I'm just bitter," Justin says. I start to speak but he laughs. "No really. She is obviously a good friend to you. But just promise me you won't do anything you don't want to do just because she asks it of you."

"She wouldn't do that," I say.

"So, there's no reason you can't promise me then," he says and logically, I can't argue with that one and so I find myself nodding my head.

"I promise," I say.

"Good enough for me," Justin says. He stands up. "Let me

go and get us some shots. It's not a celebration without a tequila shot or two, is it?"

I laugh and shake my head. I would normally say no to a shot when I'm already feeling quite drunk, but after the conversation about Louisa, it's nice to be back laughing and joking and I don't want to say no and start another awkward moment between us.

While it's annoyed me a bit that Justin can't see the good in Louisa and what a good friend she has been to me, I must admit I also think it's kind of sweet that Justin has my back like that and tries to look out for me if he thinks someone is using me. He really is a good friend to me too, just in a different way. Still though, I look at him now and I really can't see what I found attractive about him before.

Don't get me wrong, he's far from ugly or anything like that. He's tall and he has a nice physique and a tan. He has jet black hair which he wears longish, gelled back off his face. He is always dressed in the latest fashion, most often designers I could only dream of wearing, and I think maybe that's the problem. He's kind of showy and that's really not me. I also think now that he's a bit too pretty for my tastes. That's the difference between him and Luke. Justin is pretty in an almost feminine way, but Luke is handsome in like a rugged, manly way.

I tell myself to stop thinking about Luke. Nothing can ever happen and now I won't even be working directly beneath him so I will likely not even see him around much, and I can let my crush on him go. It feels like more than a crush though. When I think of myself not seeing him around much, it feels like there's a hole in me that only he can fill. I tell myself I'm being melodramatic, that I'm only thinking this way because I have been drinking, but I really don't believe that's the case for a second.

# CHAPTER
## *Fourteen*

## LUKE

It's been three weeks since Louisa went to work on the web development team. I would like to say I don't think about her much at all now, and that the time has passed in the normal way. But if I did that, I would be lying. The time has dragged so much when my day isn't broken up with little sightings of her and I haven't stopped thinking about her. If anything, I believe that I actually think about her more now I don't get to see her all of the time.

I wake up on a morning and I imagine how it would be waking up next to Louisa, how her slim warm body would feel in my arms as I fucked her. I imagine how it would be having her sneak into my office through the working day and steal kisses and more. And I imagine what evenings would be like, where I would lay her down on my bed and eat her out and make her come until she is begging me to fuck her, and then I would oblige her and make her come again. Thinking like that never fails to make my cock hard for her and at home, I jerk off, imagining that my hand is her hand, picturing her gorgeous face, her small, perky breasts. But at work, it isn't something I can do anything about except stay behind my desk and hope no one has a reasonable request for me to stand up. So far, I haven't been caught, but it's only a matter of time before it happens. No one will know it's because I'm thinking of Louisa, but it will still be embarrassing enough on its own. I have got to get her out of my head before that can be allowed to happen.

That's going to be even harder than usual for the next few minutes, because I have Karl scheduled to come up to my office and give me the weekly update on Louisa's progress within his team. So far, Karl has reported that she's fitting in well and she has completed everything he has asked her to do to a high standard. This week, he's letting her have a bit more freedom and I'm interested to know how that's gone. If she's going to revert to the image Enrique painted of her, then it's going to be now when she thinks no one is holding her reins.

Karl arrives for the meeting and sits down. We chat for a bit and then I move the conversation around to the reason he's here.

"How are things going with Louisa?" I ask.

"Take a look for yourself," Karl says. He nods towards my computer. "May I?"

"Go ahead," I say.

He swivels the screen around to face him and then he turns the keyboard around and after a few seconds of him clicking around and his fingers dancing over the keys, he turns the screen back to face me. He is showing me a mock-up of one of the screens from the app. Everything is exactly as we discussed, and it looks perfectly fine, but I wouldn't expect any less from anyone who has a degree in web development. It's not that Louisa isn't doing her job – she is – I just expected more with Karl wanting to show me the page instead of just saying she had completed it to a high standard or whatever. It turns out he isn't finished yet though.

"That's pretty good, isn't it?" Karl says and I nod. "Keep it in mind while I show you this."

He turns his focus back to the computer for a moment and then he turns the screen back towards me again. The screen shows the same page, but a different version of it. The color scheme fits everything we discussed, but the fonts are different, and the images used aren't of the aesthetic that we discussed either. It's edgier and I have to admit I prefer it. But I don't see what it has to do with Louisa's progress. But then again, Karl isn't obsessed with her like I am, and he might be taking this opportunity while he has my attention to ask my thoughts on changing direction slightly with the look of the app.

"What do you think?" he asks.

"I prefer the second one. I know it's not what we signed off on, but seeing it against our original idea, it kind of makes our original one look a little bit drab," I say. "Do you prefer the second one, or the original one?"

"The second one by a country mile. If you are in agreement, I'm going to have a team meeting later on today and brief the team on the changes and what we are aiming for going forward," he says.

"I am in agreement," I say.

Karl nods but he doesn't volunteer any information about Louisa so I guess I will have to bring it up.

"So, Louisa then? How's she coming along?" I ask. "Has she impressed you now that she is working with less hand holding?"

"I guess I didn't make it clear. The first layout of the app page was Louisa's work following the template I gave her," Karl says, and I nod. I did understand that, but as good as it is, it's hardly her having free reign. "The second layout of the app page was Louisa – in her words – just trying something to see if I liked it."

My eyes open wider. He was right. He hadn't made that clear at all. In fact, I'm still not sure I have understood correctly.

"Wait. You're telling me Louisa did that second layout without any input from you or the team?" I say. "And now we're basing the look of our whole app on her idea?"

Karl grins and nods his head.

"Yes. That's exactly what I'm saying. I know it's early days yet, but if you want my opinion on this woman, I say forget the internship. Give her a permanent contract now before she has a chance to look around and slip away," Karl says.

"She already has an offer on the table," I say.

"Then find out what it is and beat it," Karl says.

Once we have finished our discussion – where he confirms that spoiled and lazy are words he would not associate with Louisa in any way - and he has left the office, I find myself thinking about what he said about finding out what her offer is and beating it to keep her here. Would she consider staying? Would Enrique be happy if I did that? Who would I approach first? Her or him? It's all too complicated to work through at the minute and I decide to shelve the idea for now. I will try and have a conversation or two with Louisa where I hint at the idea of her staying here and see how she reacts and then go from there. There's no point in me putting the feelers out with Enrique about it if Louisa doesn't want to work here. It will just risk causing trouble for their family for no reason.

I cross the lobby heading for the elevator after lunch. I call the elevator and get in. I hit the button for the fifth floor, and then I hear running feet behind me, and I press the hold button. I turn as someone else bursts into the elevator and gives me a breathless thank you. I feel my cock twitching when I see the person is Louisa.

"What floor?" I say, managing to sound normal.

"Four please," she says. "Karl has called a team meeting in one of the smaller conference rooms."

I nod and hit the button for the fourth floor and the doors close.

"So how is life in web development?" I ask.

"It's good," Louisa says. She looks so enthusiastic when she speaks, it's obvious she loves the work. Her cheeks flush slightly and she can't stop herself from smiling. Her enthusiasm is infectious, and I find myself smiling back at her. "I love the work so much and the team is all lovely and welcoming."

"But ...?" I say. "Because there's always a but."

I'm only joking, but Louisa looks at me and she's serious now.

"But I miss you," she blurts out. The slight pink hint of her cheeks darkens to red. "I mean ... I miss working with you ... for you. You know what I mean."

I smile and it does nothing to help Louisa regain her composure.

"I know exactly what you mean. And for what it's worth, I miss having you around too," I say.

"You only miss me bringing you coffee," she jokes and then the elevator reaches her floor, and the doors ping open, and she steps out.

The doors start to close.

"Actually, Rachel brings me twice as many cups a day," I say. "But the view isn't as good."

The doors close before she can turn around or reply to me, but I know she heard me, and I just have to hope I didn't cross a line. I definitely get vibes from her that she is attracted to me and whenever I have flirted with her, she has always joined in. I don't think I have anything to worry about that way.

The elevator reaches my floor and as I walk towards my office, my cell phone pings in my pocket. I pull it out and smile when I see I have a text message from Louisa.

"It's good to hear that you enjoyed the view," the text message says, and I grin to myself. She is into me. I knew it. But nothing has changed. She's still Enrique's daughter and doing anything about the way I feel towards her is still massively unprofessional.

I get back to my office and sit down and ponder for a moment. I suppose the time she's got left here isn't that long. Two months and one week. And once she's left here, it wouldn't be unprofessional to date her, and I can't see why Enrique would have a problem with it when she's not working for me. But then I think of the work she's doing and Karl saying we need to keep her here. That's what would be best for the company, and I could make it the best option for Louisa by giving her a good offer. But then I can never be with her. I sigh and decide the only thing to do is put her out of my mind. It's easier said than done, but what's the point of torturing myself with thoughts of being with someone that I know I can't let myself have.

My cell phone pings again, and I see it's Louisa again. I open the message and smile.

"What's wrong? Have you gone all shy?" her text message reads.

Oh, fuck it, I think to myself, and I type out a reply.

"Actually, I was just wondering which bar to take you to tonight for a drink to officially welcome you to the company," I write back.

We both know it's far too late for that, and I'm sure Louisa is bright enough to know that wording it that way is a get out of jail free card for me so if she says no, she's not rejecting the idea of a night with me, just saying no to drinks with the boss as such. I need not have bothered covering my bases because her positive reply pings through almost instantly.

"Meeting is starting. Text me the time and place and I'll be there."

I smile and send her a text back to meet at eight at my local. I give her the address of the place in case she doesn't know where it is and then I force myself to focus on my work for the rest of the day. I manage to get a fair bit done somehow, but I do it all with a smile on my face and half a mind on Louisa and where tonight might end up going.

# CHAPTER

## Fifteen

**LUKE**

I take a quick look at my reflection in the window of the bar as I pass it. I'm wearing a pair of black jeans, and a blue, short sleeved t shirt. I wanted to look presentable, but not like I was dressed too over the top, and I think I hit the level I was going for. I am wearing my most expensive cologne though.

I reach the door of the bar and pull it open. The place isn't packed, but it isn't empty either. It has a nice ambience about it where it feels like it's quiet enough to talk but loud enough not to be overheard. I spot Louisa sitting on a bar stool with a glass of something in front of her and I make my way across the as yet empty dance floor.

Louisa turns her head in my direction as I step up beside her at the bar.

"Hi," she says. "Should we get a table?"

"Wow," I reply, looking at her as she slips off the stool.

She's wearing a short black playsuit with printed daisies on it and brown wedges. She has a yellow bag slung across her body. She is wearing her hair half up and half down. The down half is in beachy curls, and I have to physically stop myself from reaching out and running my fingers through it.

"Nice answer," she says. She smiles and then looks down as though she's almost afraid to make eye contact with me.

"What can I get you?" the bartender says to me.

"Scotch on the rocks please," I say. I look at Louisa. "What are you having?"

"A gin and tonic please," she says.

I nod to the bartender, and he fixes the drinks while Louisa goes to get us a table. I watch her walk away. The playsuit isn't particularly tight fitting, but it does cut in at her waist and it makes me want to rest my hands there as I kiss her.

Louisa chooses a table – a good choice in my mind. It's not too close to anyone else, but it's not like in a dark little corner somewhere which would be a very different vibe to drinks with the boss, which at the moment, I assume we are still pretending this is.

I pay for the drinks and go to the table and sit down. Louisa thanks me for the drink and takes a sip.

I pick up my own drink and raise my glass.

"Welcome to the company," I say.

"Thanks," Louisa says, tapping her glass against mine.

We both drink and I decide to put out the feelers about her maybe staying on. It's a safe topic compared to what I would like to say to her, and it is an opening into a real conversation hopefully.

"Karl is very pleased with your work," I say. "He showed me the app page you designed, and I am too."

"Thank you," she says. She smiles playfully. "See I can do things other than filing you know."

"I didn't doubt it," I say.

Louisa snorts out a laugh.

"Bullshit," she says.

"Ok, you got me. I did doubt it. But you as sure as hell proved me wrong on that one," I say.

"I hope that means I'll be getting a good reference," Louisa says.

"Or maybe I'll give you an awful reference so no one wants to hire you, and we can keep you," I say with a laugh.

She gave me the perfect lead in there and I had to take it. She laughs too but she doesn't say whether she would actually like to stay or not and I don't want to push her.

"You make it sound like you're going to lock me away in a tower somewhere," she jokes.

"You'd better be on your best behavior, or I just might," I fire back.

"I can do that, but something tells me you would prefer the naughty side of me," Louisa says.

"I can't imagine why you have that impression of me," I reply.

Louisa laughs softly and takes a drink. I watch her throat work as she swallows it. She sees me watching her and smiles self-consciously.

"What? Do I have something on my face?" she says.

I shake my head. I force myself to look away. Flirting is one thing, but I don't want to make her uncomfortable or come across as a creep.

"What made you decide to go into web development?" I ask.

"I was always quite creative growing up, but I wasn't a good drawer or painter or anything like that. I tried graphic design, but again, I wasn't a great drawer, and my stuff never came out like how I saw it my head. I discovered web development as an accidental side line to that really. I discovered I liked playing around with other people's graphics and fonts and putting them together in new ways. From there, I learned to code so I could do it without it looking like a bad photoshop job. I had several friends ask me to work on websites for them and word of mouth reached a few local businesses and they paid me to design websites for them and that's when I realized there was a potential career in it."

"I suppose I could have left college and started my own business doing that kind of thing, but I felt like that wasn't what I wanted. I think running a business is great if that's your thing, but for me, it would mean that I had to do a thousand and one tasks I didn't want to do and less and less hands-on work. So, I decided to get my degree and go down that route, but with the aim of working for a company."

She finishes up and takes another sip of her drink.

"How about you? What made you start Sold?" she asks.

"I was the opposite of you," I say with a smile. "I knew from quite early on that I wanted to run my own business. I didn't know what I would do at first, but I knew I didn't want to work for someone else. I got the idea for Sold when I started to use eBay as part of a retail business I tried. I found it to be a good tool for the most part – certainly the best available at the time - but there were lots of things I felt would work better a different way and the more I used the site, the more strongly I felt about it and so I decided to start Sold. I talked to potential investors, and they believed in me and my ideas, and I got enough money together to make it happen. I hired people to build a website that worked faster and smarter than the alternatives, and one that had more focus on the sellers. After all, they are our clients really, and I find that eBay in particular put way too much focus on siding with buyers, even when the seller can prove the buyer is lying. I was lucky – I got into the market at just the right time and Sold just took off."

"I think it was likely more than luck," Louisa says. "The timing obviously was right which helped, but it sounds like a hell of a lot of work at the beginning and that's not luck, that's determination and a damned good idea."

"Maybe a bit of that too," I say.

"So, you're the sort of man who sees what he wants and goes for it then?" Louisa says, not meeting my eye.

"Yes and no," I say. "I like to bide my time. When the right moment comes along, then I will go after what I want, but sometimes, I have found myself wanting something and the time isn't right, so I hold back."

"Is that why you've never gotten married?" Louisa asks me.

It's a jump to the personal and I'm a little bit surprised by it, but I have nothing to hide, and I am quite open to answering her.

"I haven't purposely avoided marriage, I just haven't found the right person yet," I say. "I guess I will when the time is right for that too. But how do you know I'm not married or haven't been divorced?"

"I looked you up online," Louisa says.

I expect her to blush or at least look a bit sheepish at this confession, but she's completely unfazed by the admission. Because I like her, I suppose I don't mind the idea of her looking me up, but if I didn't, would I find it weird? Maybe a little bit.

"Stalker much," I say, making light of it but letting her know she's very close to crossing a line.

"Hardly," she says. "Don't tell me you never look potential employees up online. Or if not you personally, then your HR department?"

"Sure," I say. "We look for red flags, but not their relationship status."

"And people who are about to start working for someone generally do the same thing. Look them up, find out a bit about them, see if they are someone they can work well with.

But you have to be the awkward one and not be on LinkedIn, so I had to resort to looking you up on Facebook, where your relationship status is at the top of your profile and pretty hard to miss," she says.

"Ok, fair enough," I say. "So do you think I should set myself up a LinkedIn profile, even though I'm not looking for a career change or anything like that?"

Louisa shrugs one shoulder.

"It won't hurt," she says. "If nothing else, it means that anyone who is considering a role at the company will have somewhere to look you up without seeming like a stalker."

We both laugh and I file that idea away for another day. Maybe I will make myself a profile, but at the very least, I am going to tighten my privacy settings on Facebook. Louisa is one thing, but I don't like the idea of any random person being about to find out details about me and my life so easily.

"Same again," I say, nodding to Louisa's almost empty glass.

"Let me get these," she says.

"Stop it," I say. "What sort of a welcome to the company would that be?"

She smiles and nods her head.

"Same again then please," she relents.

I go to the bar and get us both another drink and then I go back to the table, and we spend the rest of the night chatting and laughing and flirting. Before long, it doesn't feel like I'm a boss taking a new employee out for welcome drinks. It feels like we're friends on a night out, friends that share a lot of chemistry and are waiting for the right moment to take their relationship to the next level.

Is tonight the right moment though? Everything feels right except for the fact that Louisa works for me and of course her father is on the board. If it wasn't for those two little details, I would say tonight was the night. To be perfectly honest, if I didn't need Enrique's backing for my new idea, I would go for it tonight and throw caution to the wind. Plenty of people manage to date and work together and it's not like I am Louisa's direct boss. I'm sure we could make it work. But that isn't the situation, and I guess I will have to do like I did with my business – wait for the right moment, because if I do jump in to early, I'm risking ruining something that could be really good. I hope Louisa has worked out that when I was talking about timing and waiting for the right moment, that I was letting her know that moment will come for us.

Waiting won't be easy though, and every time Louisa giggles at my jokes, or looks me in the eye and bites her lip, or touches her hair or my arm, I feel it getting harder and harder to wait.

When the bell goes for last orders, I'm shocked to hear it. The night has flown by, and Louisa seems as surprised by the late hour as I am.

"It can't be that time already," she says.

I check my watch and nod.

"It is," I say, and we both laugh. "Would you like me to call you a cab?"

"Yes please," Louisa says. "I'll just use the ladies' room while you do it."

I watch her walk away from the table and I call her a cab. She comes back to the table, and we drain the last of our drinks.

"The cab driver said it won't be long, so should we wait outside?" I say.

"Ok," Louisa says.

We leave the table and walk across the bar.; I open the door for Louisa. She steps outside and I follow her. It's a warm enough evening and it actually feels nice to get a bit of fresh air. I lean back against the wall and Louisa stands facing me, a couple of feet between us.

"Thank you for tonight," she says. "I really enjoyed it."

"Well, that was never in doubt was it when you get to spend the night with someone as charming as me," I say with a grin.

"Ah that must be it then," she says, grinning back at me.

"I enjoyed it too," I say. "So, you must be a bit of a charmer yourself."

"I can be when the moment calls for it," she says.

"And do you think this moment calls for it?" I ask.

"No," she says. "I think this moment calls for something else."

I start to ask her what, but she closes the gap between us, and the next thing I know, her lips are on mine. I most certainly did not see that coming, but I'm also not complaining. All my reasons why this can't happen go out of the window now that it is happening, and I wrap my arms around Louisa and pull her against me. She pushes her hands into my hair as our kiss becomes more passionate. Our tongues collide as our lips mash together, the perfect fit.

I have to say, as kisses go, this one is mind blowing. My whole body comes alive as we kiss, and my cock hardens, ready for Louisa to take it inside of her so I can rock both of our worlds. Of course, this isn't the time or the place for it and I pull back slightly so she can't feel my hardness against her.

She doesn't seem to notice me pulling my hips back slightly as she moans into my mouth and kisses me harder, faster, and more passionately than I think I have ever been kissed.

I never want this kiss to end, but end it must, and we come apart at the sound of a car pulling up beside us. I glance over Louisa's shoulder and the driver gives me a thumb's up, which I hope means he is our cab driver rather than that he is enjoying the show.

# CHAPTER
## Sixteen

TIA

What the hell have I done?

The night has been lovely. I have enjoyed every minute of it. Luke is so different outside of the office. He still has that quiet confidence and somehow, being with him makes me feel safe, but he is much less reserved than he is at work. We have spent the whole night laughing, teasing each other, and flirting. I knew I was on dangerous ground with that, but I really like him, and I couldn't help but get caught up in the moment with him. Why the fuck did I have to pretend to be Louisa?

In hindsight, it was a bad move, but it's done now, and I can hardly just rock up and tell the truth now. I should never have kissed Luke. It doesn't matter that it was the sort of kiss I have only ever dreamed of before now. It doesn't matter that my pussy was instantly wet for him and that my clit is still tingling now at the thought of the kiss. It doesn't matter that I want to throw him on the ground and ride him. What matters is that I can't do any of that and I was the one to instigate the kiss which makes it even worse, but I have to say something. I have to let Luke know we can't do that again.

I'm aware of the cab behind me, waiting for me to get in, but this has to come first. I can't not say this now, because if I don't say it now, I don't think I'll have the courage to say it later and … For fuck's sake, why is everything such a fucking mess? Urgh.

"Shit, Luke, I'm so sorry. I don't know what came over me. Please forgive me," I say.

"Don't worry, there's nothing to forgive," Luke says. "Mistakes happen. And yes, it was a fun mistake, but that doesn't mean we have to repeat it."

"Thank you for not making this more awkward than it already is," I say.

I'm partly relieved that he has taken it so well, but there is a part of me that is kind of gutted. That part of me wanted him to tell me it wasn't a mistake and that it most definitely will happen again. Maybe if he had chosen to fight for me a little bit, I could convince myself my name doesn't matter. Because that's the only part of me that's fake. The rest is all me. And once my internship is up, I can tell Luke the truth, and maybe he'll just laugh about it. But now all of that is off the table because he thinks the kiss was a mistake too. A nice mistake as he put it, but still a mistake.

"Good night, Louisa," Luke says, and I take my cue and get into the cab, looking back over my shoulder and giving him one last sad smile before I do.

I give the cab driver my address and he puts the car into drive and pulls away and heads off towards my building. I look out of the window, watching the buildings pass me by, but I'm not seeing them. Not really. Instead, I'm back outside of the bar, and I'm kissing Luke, and he is kissing me back and everything is perfect. And when I say it's a mistake and apologize, he tells me that's not true, and he pulls me in and kisses me again.

All the way home, all of the time I'm getting ready for bed, and all of the time I spend trying to drift off to sleep, I'm thinking of Luke and specifically, that kiss. The way I felt inside when we kissed is like nothing I have ever felt before and I want – no I need – to feel that way again. That kiss has awoken something inside of me, something that had no right to be awake, and I know that what I feel for Luke is way more than a crush. I am in so much trouble here, because I have allowed myself to fall way too deep into something that can never even happen, with someone who doesn't want it to happen. Isn't that just a great ending to the night.

# CHAPTER
## *Seventeen*

## LUKE

I walk into the lobby and the first person I see is Louisa. I was determined to let last night go and be professional, but looking at her now, I don't think I can do that. Us kissing wasn't a mistake. I don't know why Louisa said it was, because no one kisses someone like that if they aren't feeling it. Maybe she panicked that I wasn't into her and said it hoping I would argue the point. I agreed that it was a mistake because I was still telling myself it couldn't happen but fuck it. I don't care that her father is on the board of directors anymore, and if me being with his daughter means he votes against me, then so be it, because that woman is going to be mine.

I start towards her, but then I realize that she isn't alone, and the man she's walking with isn't a member of my staff. He could be someone from one of the other companies in the building, but I don't recognize him at all and as Louisa reaches the elevator, the man kisses her on the cheek and turns to leave. So, he doesn't work here then.

I feel anger swirling inside of me at the thought of someone else getting to touch Louisa, getting to kiss her and hold her. What the fuck? Is this why she said our kiss was a mistake? Because she has a boyfriend? The thought sends another spear of anger through me, and I force myself to think about something else before I really lose my temper and make a fool of myself right here in the lobby.

I can't shake off my anger. I have felt it all day since I saw that bastard kiss my woman. Yes, it was only her cheek, but it still has me reeling. I know Louisa has done nothing wrong really, but I feel like she has betrayed me.

At no point did she tell me she was single and even the kiss is really a betrayal of her boyfriend, not me. Maybe I could argue that she led me on a bit, but maybe she thought the flirting we were doing was just in fun.

Nothing I tell myself helps though. It doesn't make me any less pissed off, and it doesn't make me any less interested in being with Louisa. Boyfriend or no boyfriend, I want that woman, hell I need that woman. This has gone way beyond lust; last night I felt like we really connected on a level beyond that. And seeing her this morning just cemented that idea.

There's a knock on my office door, and I shout come in, pleased that there is going to be a distraction from my thoughts of Louisa. The door opens and it seems that it won't be a distraction after all as Louisa herself walks in.

She looks every bit as good as she always does, and I know I can't let her walk away. But what can I do? I can't actually force her to leave her boyfriend. Or maybe I can. We'd be so good together. She should be with me.

"Sit down," I say, and Louisa does. "What can I do for you?"

She lifts up her hand and puts a sheet of paper I hadn't noticed on my desk.

"Karl asked me to bring this to you and have you review it and sign it," she says. "He says it's too important to sit on the receptionist's desk forgotten in some in tray."

"Does he now?" I snap. "And since when did he start calling the shots and telling me what to do?"

Louisa squirms in her seat looking visibly uncomfortable and I instantly regret snapping at her. I remind myself again that she hasn't done anything to justify me being a dick to her, and especially in this scenario. If I am to be mad at anyone for this, it should be Karl. The fact I'm not mad at Karl tells me it's personal and I don't want to bring that to the office.

"Sorry," I grunt. "I realize you're just the messenger."

She looks a bit more relaxed at that and as much as I didn't much like saying it, I feel like it was the right thing to do, and I'm glad Louisa looks a bit more comfortable.

# CHAPTER
## Eighteen

**TIA**

I was so nervous when I had to come to Luke's office. When Karl asked me to run the document up to him and that I had to have him look at it personally right now, I came so close to asking him to send someone else. But he would obviously ask why, and other than the truth, I couldn't think of anything I could say that would sound plausible and not make it look like I couldn't be bothered to do my job. And I certainly wasn't about to tell him the truth or have him think I was being lazy.

I suppose in a way though, it's good that Luke and I are being forced to see each other today. I feel like the longer it goes between us without us seeing each other again, the more awkward it would be. This is bad enough and it hasn't even been twelve hours.

I really don't think Luke snapped at me because of Karl's request. I don't think Karl would have sent me without a warning if that was something that was likely to happen. I think it's because he's pissed off that I kissed him, but he doesn't want to seem like he's being a dick about it. At least he's apologized now though and is looking over the sheet. Hopefully he will just sign it and hand it back to me and this will be over.

Of course that doesn't happen though, because it's Luke and since when has he done anything the easy way. He does read and sign the document, but he keeps it out of my reach while he studies my face. His gaze is intense, and I blush, but I can't bring myself to look away, it's like he has me mesmerized.

"You must feel like playing messenger is quite a come down after being let loose on the app," Luke says when he finally breaks eye contact with me.

His eyes flash with humor and I'm pretty sure he's teasing me. I like that. It feels like we can just go back to being normal with each other again.

"The joys of being an intern I guess," I say with an unsure smile. Luke smiles back at me and my uncertainty falls away and my smile widens. "I much prefer the app work though."

"I would hope so," Luke says. "When you have a choice of two things, always choose the superior one."

The way he looks at me when he says it tells me that he is no longer talking about choosing a favorite task, but I have no idea what he's referring to, and there's no way I am going to ask him and risk this rather precarious normalcy between us fading back away into awkwardness. I don't want to just ignore what he has said either and I choose to answer in the way I would have this time yesterday. That feels safest.

"But what if I choose the option that I feel is superior and other people think I chose the worst option?" I say.

"Well, I think most people would say follow your heart. Me, I say make sure you make the right choice, and no one will disagree with you," Luke says.

"And do you disagree with me? Do you believe running errands is better than web development work?" I say.

"Maybe not running errands per se, but you get to come and see me so there's that," he says.

"Yes, that does make it a little bit tougher. But tough enough? I'm not sure, because I could choose web development work and then see you in the pub again," I laugh.

"Good point," Luke says. "But what if your boyfriend wants to see you the same night that I want to take you to the pub? Who do you choose then?"

"I don't have a boyfriend, so I can't really answer that one. I guess I could think about it hypothetically," I reply.

"I saw you," Luke says, and the gentle playfulness has gone from his voice as he looks at me with the piercing gaze I can't look away from once more. "In the lobby this morning."

I have no idea where he is going with this or how the conversation has jumped here, but then I remember. I had breakfast with Justin this morning, and he insisted on walking me to work. Not just to the door either, but to the elevator.

"Ah, then I guess you saw me with Justin," I say. "He's not my boyfriend. He's just a friend."

Should I mention the fact he's my ex-boyfriend? I decide not to. It's not at all relevant and I'm not lying. Justin is my friend now and nothing more.

"That's good," Luke says.

"Is it?" I say, barely able to breathe as I stare into Luke's eyes.

"Yes. Because you are going to be mine. And you having a boyfriend would complicate that," he says.

What do I even say to that? On the one hand, I feel like I should object to him claiming me like I'm some sort of object, but on the other hand, hearing him say I am going to be his like it is a foregone conclusion makes my pussy dampen and makes me want him all the more.

Ok, so I won't do a feminist rant, but I have to say something. He's obviously waiting for an answer, and I'm just sitting here staring at him. His desk phone rings and breaks the moment and Luke looks away from me finally and I can move and think and function again.

He slides the sheet of paper for Karl back across to me as he takes the call, and I realize I'm being dismissed. I get up and leave Luke's office and as I close the door gently behind me, I feel my face break into a smile that is so big it hurts my cheeks. I feel like dancing and singing and screaming in delight. But I try to reel myself back in, because I can't be reading this correctly, can I? I must have misheard or misunderstood, because surely there's no way Luke just announced I am going to be his.

And even if he did, nothing has changed. I still can't do it. I'm still hiding my identity. But then again, if he insists on us being together right now, then when the internship is over and I come clean, can he really blame only me? It's like he said about his business. It's all about timing. It's the wrong time for me to tell him I'm really Tia, but that doesn't mean it's the wrong time to give myself to Luke completely. After all, what is a name when I'm willing to give him my body, my mind and my soul?

# CHAPTER
## Nineteen

**TIA**

I'm humming to myself as I work on the latest tweaks for Karl. We have had a meeting and everything we have done so far has been analysed and any required changes have been noted down, and making those changes fell to me. It means going through thousands of lines of code, often just to change one or two characters and make changes on the page that to the untrained eye might seem pointless, but to a techie makes a big difference. The tweaks I have to make will likely take at least a week, but I decided to work late tonight and at least make a decent start on them.

I suppose it's fair to say it is quite a come down from having my designs accepted as the template for the app's pages, but realistically, what I'm doing now is more of an intern's job and me happening to do a design that I had the confidence to show Karl and that he and everyone else loved is the anomaly. A good anomaly. Brilliant in fact. But an anomaly all the same.

I find the character on the line I'm looking for and change it to the new agreed upon character and I tick it off my list and move on to the next one. I work steadily away and after a few hours, I have made a decent start on the work, and I don't feel so bad about the thought of coming in to it first thing in the morning now that I have already found my rhythm.

I save my work and come out of the program and then I start to close down the laptop. It's only then that it occurs to me how creepy it is here. I can work anywhere with my laptop, and I decided to just stay in the meeting room rather than go back down to the web development room because everyone else on the team was going home for the day anyway, so it made no difference to me where I sat. It sort of does now though. I'm sure if I'd gone back to the team room, there would be other people somewhere on the floor, but the fourth floor where I am is deserted except for me because it's no one's permanent place of work.

I tell myself to stop being ridiculous. If there is no one here but me, then what the hell am I afraid of? It's not like I'm going to go mental and attack myself. I don't feel one hundred percent better for that thought, but I do feel a bit better, and I even smile to myself at the thought of me attacking myself on the otherwise empty floor.

I'm still pleased when my laptop is shut down though and I slip it into its carry case. I stand up quickly and retrieve my purse from beside my chair and my jacket from the back of it. I put the jacket on, put my purse on my shoulder and pick up the laptop bag and I head for the door.

I slip out of the room into the now dimly lit corridor. The main lights have gone off and it is lit only by the emergency light which casts an eerie green glow over the walls and floor. I close the door quietly behind me and head towards the elevator. I'm a little over halfway there when I hear what sounds like footsteps behind me. I feel my heart start to race, and my mouth goes dry. I walk faster.

As I walk, I tell myself I'm being ridiculous. There is no one up here but me and I haven't heard anything except the echoes of my own paranoia. Even as I tell myself this, I'm still aware of the sound and I risk a glance over my shoulder, ready to see another member of staff also working late and then laughing to myself about it, but the hallway behind me is empty for as far as I can see.

I reach the elevator and press the call button. I stand, shifting from foot to foot, as I watch the red numbers go up as the elevator car comes to my call. It seems slower than usual, and I swear I can hear laughter, but I know that's just my own imagination. It has to be. I'm considering making a dash for the stairs when I hear the footsteps behind me again, this time loud enough that I can't pretend I'm being paranoid. I want to look back, but I just can't do it. I'm too afraid of what I might see, or worse, what I don't see but can still hear them creeping closer and closer to me.

Before I have decided if it's best to remain here or run for the stairs, the elevator car arrives, and the doors open with a ping. I practically jump into the car, and I jab the ground floor button. The doors start to close behind me, and I will them to close faster as the footsteps become faster.

"Louisa. Hold the door," a voice says, and I dare to look up and I see that it's Luke.

I press the hold button, and the doors reopen and stay that way as Luke hurries towards me. I feel my panic floating away, leaving behind a sense of relief that makes me feel like laughing. Luke reaches the elevator car and gets in and I release the hold button.

"The lobby?" I ask and he nods his head, and I jab the button again and the doors start to close.

"You gave me quite a scare there," I say. "I thought I was alone on this floor, and I heard your footsteps."

I laugh as I say it and Luke grins.

"Sorry," he says. "I had a meeting down here earlier and I left my jacket behind. I came to collect it on the way out."

"That's …" I start to say.

I'm going to say something about the timing, that he came for his jacket at the moment I was leaving, but the elevator screeching to a stop and the lights going off stop me dead in my tracks. It is pitch black and another screech makes me think we are falling, and I can't help but let out a small scream.

I feel a warm hand on the small of my back and I scream again and try to bat the hand away. It stays in place and another hand appears on my back and I'm wrapped in Luke's arms, pressed against his chest.

"It's ok," he says. "Don't panic. The elevator broke down, that's all."

His words soothe me for the most part. My heart still races but I'm not entirely sure that's from fear now. I concentrate on breathing normally, taking in Luke's scent and the calmer I become, the more I relax into Luke until I have my arms around him too.

Unexpectedly, there is a pinging sound, and the emergency lights in the elevator car switch on. Again, I find myself in a place bathed in that sickly green light, but this time, I feel no fear. In Luke's arms, I feel safe and even though the lights are back on now, I make no effort to move away from him and he seems equally happy to remain holding me.

Luke reaches up with one hand and gently strokes my cheek. I tilt my head back to look up at him and his face comes down towards mine, and my whole body comes to life. I am no longer afraid, but my body is still thrumming with adrenaline and when Luke kisses me, I feel like his lips are somehow touching every part of me at once, making that adrenaline flood my body with the most amazing tingling sensation.

# CHAPTER

## *Twenty*

**LUKE**

Louisa looks up at me, her lips parted slightly and her eyes wide open. I don't mean to kiss her, I just find myself moving closer and before I know it, my lips are on hers. She kisses me back as hungrily as I kiss her, and our hands roam over each other's bodies. I want to strip Louisa and slowly tease her, making her come with my fingers and my tongue before I fuck her, but this isn't the time or the place for that and instead, I reach down and pull her dress up over her hips.

At the same time, she fumbles my pants open and pushes them down along with my boxer shorts. She takes hold of my cock and moans into my mouth as she runs her hand along it and feels how hard it is. Her touch on my cock feels amazing, and I would happily stand here all night and have her touch me like that, but again, I'm aware that the elevator could start moving again at any time and so I gently move her hand away and then I cup her ass and lift her up.

Louisa wraps her legs around my waist and pushes her hands into my hair, her tongue delving deeper into my mouth and swirling around. I push her panties to one side and push my cock against her opening. I push inside of her in one sure stroke, and she moves her lips from mine and gasps as I enter her, stretching her and claiming her.

I move to the side of the elevator car and press her up against the wall and then I fuck her like I have been unleashed. I slam into her and pull almost all of the way out of her, and then I slam in again. I repeat the motion as Louisa matches my movements with her hips. I watch her as she comes undone. She closes her eyes, and her mouth opens in a silent O.

She moves her hands through my hair and onto my shoulders and her nails dig into the top of my back where she grips me as her face contorts with the power of her climax. I feel her already tight pussy squeeze my cock and the warmth of her and the pressure she puts on my cock gets to me and Louisa isn't the only one coming. I feel my climax in my cock and balls, but not just there. It goes up into my stomach and for a moment, I swear I can feel pleasure in every bit of my body.

It's over sooner than I want it to be and as I slip out of Louisa, I already want to be back inside of her. She unwraps her legs from around me, allowing them to drop down and she's once again standing on her feet, although she's still pressed against the wall, and I'm still pinning her in place. I run my hands down her arms and hold her wrists. I lift them above her head and bring them together, pinning them in place with only one of my hands.

The other hand I bring down and cup her hip and then I kiss her again, and I run my tongue down her neck. I can feel the goose bumps scurrying across her skin and she presses herself against me and moans.

I start to push her jacket off her shoulder when a loud clang comes from just above us in the elevator shaft.

"Won't be long and we'll have you out of there. Is everyone ok?" a voice shouts and I realize one of the maintenance workers is standing on the top of the elevator car.

"Yes, all good, thanks," I call back.

I lean into Louisa and nibble on her ear lobe and then I whisper into her ear.

"Think of this as a warm up for later," I say.

I run my fingers over her clit through her lacy panties and she gasps again and then I release her and step back and bend down and pull my boxer shorts and pants up. Louisa puts her panties right and pulls her dress down.

We don't have long to wait before the elevator lurches back to life, and in the few minutes it takes to go the rest of the way down to the lobby, we keep looking at each other and then looking away, sometimes laughing, sometimes not.

When the elevator finally reaches the ground floor, it opens onto an empty lobby,

"My place?" I say to Louisa.

She nods her head, but she makes no move to follow me when I start to walk across the lobby, and I turn back to her.

"What is it?" I ask.

"I don't know. Shouldn't we wait for the maintenance man so that he knows we're out?" she says.

"Do you want to wait?" I ask and she shakes her head.

"Then there's your answer," I say. "Now come on before I have to throw you over my shoulder and carry you to my car."

She laughs and starts walking beside me.

"You wouldn't," she says.

"Don't try me," I grin, and she laughs and when I reach out for her, she ducks away, still laughing.

I let her duck out of my reach. It's harmless enough. And

when we get back to my place, she won't be going anywhere without me touching her.

# CHAPTER
## Twenty~One

**TIA**

The first thing I notice as Luke leads me through his apartment to his bedroom is that my whole apartment would fit in his open plan living room and dining area. I soon forget those thoughts though because Luke reaches the bedroom, opens the door, and leads me inside.

His bedroom is big but not enormous and at a quick glance, it is clean, tidy, and functional. Luke pushes the door closed and then he pulls me into his arms.

"Where were we?" he says.

I take one of his hands in one of mine and lift my dress up with the other one. I put his hand against my panties.

"About here I think," I remind him.

"Yes. That feels about right," he says and then his mouth is on mine, and we move towards the bed, breaking our kiss only to pull our clothes over our heads. By the time Luke pushes me gently onto his bed, we are both naked, and Luke's bedroom floor is covered in clothes.

I push myself backwards as Luke follows me onto his bed and I reach up for him and pull him down on top of me. My lips find his and we kiss passionately as my hands roam over his bare back and sides and down to his ass. I knead his ass cheeks in my hands and then I move one hand around and push it between our bodies. I go for Luke's cock, wanting to guide it into me, but he pulls away from my touch. He takes his mouth away from mine and looks down at me. His shakes his head, his eyes glinting playfully.

"Not yet Miss Eager," he says and then he proceeds to kiss his way down my body until his head is between my thighs.

He puts his hands on my inner thighs, pushing my legs further apart and then he runs his tongue from my pussy to my clit and fire floods me. I arch my back and moan his name as he settles down with his tongue on my clit, working it side to side and back and forth. He brings me right to the edge and then he moves his tongue away, licking back through my slit. He licks around my pussy and then pushes his tongue inside of me. As he tongue fucks me, he uses his fingers on my clit and the double sensation sends me cascading over the edge.

I come hard, my hands making fists and my back coming up off the bed. I call out Luke's name as he continues to play with my clit. He pulls his tongue out of me, and he laps at the edge of my pussy, licking up my juices as they squirt out of me.

Finally, when I feel like I can't take it anymore, Luke moves his fingers away from me. The multiple orgasm I have just had is the most intense pleasure I have ever felt in my life, and despite thinking I couldn't take it for another second, now Luke is no longer touching me, I crave his touch once more. I need to feel him inside of me.

He lifts his head up and grins up at me, wiping my juices from his gleaming wet face with the back of one hand. He leans down and kisses his way back up my body, pausing at my breasts and sucking and nibbling at my nipples until they are both standing to attention, and only then does he continue to kiss up my body until he reaches my neck. He kisses his way up my throat and then our mouths come together again, and I can taste my own pleasure on Luke's tongue as our tongues collide and our lips work together as one.

I feel Luke lining his hard cock up with my pussy and the tip pushes inside of me and then stops. Luke takes his mouth from mine and looks down at me. I look up into his eyes as they darken with lust, and he pushes all of the way into me.

"You," he says on the first thrust.

He pulls out and pushes into me again.

"Are."

Again, he pulls out and then fills me up once more.

"Mine," he finishes.

I nod. Yes. I am his. I see now that from the moment we met, me being his was inevitable - we have just been moving towards this moment.

"Say it," Luke says, his cock all of the way up me, stretching me and making me accommodate his huge girth.

"I am yours," I say, gasping as he starts to thrust again. "I am yours."

"That's right," he says and then he's thrusting into me hard and fast, and I'm clinging to him, matching his thrusts with my own, greedy for another orgasm.

Luke pulls out of me and sits back on his heels.

"Turn over," he commands, and I rush to do as he says. I get onto my front. "Up on all fours."

Again, I do as he says and once I'm in position, he fills me up again. He puts his hands on my hips, pulling me back against him with each thrust. I can feel his cock banging off my cervix. It is a little bit painful at first, but after the first few times, the pain gives way to pleasure, and I cry out Luke's name on every thrust. One of his hands comes off my hip and moves around to the front of my body and he works my clit as he fucks me.

"Oh my God yes, yes," I scream as another orgasm slams through me and rocks my world.

I feel as though I'm floating, like I'm just a ball of pleasure with no purpose other than to feel this fucking good all of the time. I try to swallow, and I can't. I try to breathe, and I can't. It only confirms that I am no longer bound by the constraints of humanity. I am just pleasure, pulsing and writhing.

Finally, Luke's fingers move back onto my hip, and I feel myself coming down. My body feels sated, and I can swallow and breathe again. My chest is burning with the lack of oxygen, and I gasp and pant, trying to get my breath back while Luke pounds into me one last time and then goes rigid as he comes.

"Fuck, Louisa," he moans as he spurts into me.

For a moment, it throws me off a little bit hearing him moan another woman's name, but I remind myself it's just a word and he obviously means me. It's me that he's thinking of as he comes. Me he's looking at. Me he's inside of. The moment passes and Luke slips out of me, and I collapse onto the mattress with him beside me.

When I feel like I can move again, I roll off my front and onto my side facing Luke. He smiles sleepily at me.

"You know that means you're mine now, right?" he says.

I nod, not trusting my voice to come out normally.

"I want to hear you say it," he says.

"I am yours," I say, and my voice doesn't betray how I feel in the moment by shaking.

Luke leans forward and kisses me.

"Damned right you are," he says.

He closes his eyes, and I want to let my eyes close too and just stay here but I remind myself of why I have to leave and it's too important to risk falling asleep and not doing it, so I sit up.

"Where are you going?" Luke mumbles sleepily from beside me.

"Home," I say.

"You don't have to go home," he says. "Just stay here."

I shake my head.

"No, I want to go home," I say.

"It's been a long week and you've worn me out completely. I don't think I have the energy to drive you home," Luke says.

"You don't have to," I say. I lean down and kiss him. "I'll get a cab."

# CHAPTER
## Twenty~Two

**LUKE**

Obviously, I'm not about to let Louisa get a cab home. Don't get me wrong, I am kind of tired and I would be happy to stay here and drift off to sleep, but I only really said that to try and talk her into staying the night. I'm not about to beg her to stay though, and I sit up and push the comforter back.

"I'm serious," Louisa says. "I really don't mind getting a cab."

I love that she really is serious, and I feel like if I said 'ok then' she wouldn't hold it against me like some girls would. Knowing that makes me even less likely to let it happen though.

"I know you don't mind, but I would mind," I say, and she stops arguing with me and continues putting her clothes on. I watch for a moment and although I much prefer them coming off, it's still a nice enough show. When she's dressed, I get up and go to my wardrobe and pull on a pair of jeans and a t shirt. I don't bother with underwear or socks or anything. It's not like I'm going to need them.

"Ready?" I ask and Louisa nods her head.

She has all of her clothes back on and she's got her purse and her laptop bag in her hand. I lead her to the door and stop to grab my keys and then we step out into the hallway, and I lock my front door. We go down the stairs and out the back door into the attached parking lot. I wait a moment to make sure the door engages and then we walk to my car. I unlock the car, and we get in and Louisa gives me her address which I put in my GPS. It's not a long drive to her place. It's not one of the nicer areas of the city, but it's far from being one of the worst and when I pull up outside of her building, I see it looks fairly new and clean and nice.

"Thanks," Louisa says as I kill the engine.

"I'll walk you up," I say.

She nods her head, and we get out of the car. She unlocks the door, and we go up a single flight of stairs and then to her apartment.

"This is me," she says, stopping outside of a door marked with a number five.

I lean down and kiss her, and she moves closer against me. My body responds to her kiss, and I can't help but deepen my kiss. Louisa gently pulls back, and I think she is going to say this was a mistake again. I won't let her do that this time. I warned her that if we fucked, she was mine and we fucked. She doesn't say we're a mistake though.

"Why don't you come in?" she says, her chest rising and falling rapidly as she looks at me. Her skin is flushed, and she looks like a porcelain doll. "You know for coffee?"

I give a breathy laugh at the last part and nod. Louisa turns in my arms and unlocks her apartment door with the key she still has out. I release her and we go inside, and she puts her keys on a small hook beside the door, followed by her laptop bag, her purse and her jacket which all go on larger hooks beside a couple of other coats.

"Do you have a roommate?" I ask, nodding towards the coats.

"No, they're mine," Louisa replies.

She kicks her shoes off and leads me to the living room.

"Sit down while I put the coffee on," she says.

"I think we both know it's not coffee I came in for," I say, and she flushes again and nods.

"The bedroom is the second door on the left," she says, pointing back out into the hallway we have just left. "I won't be a minute."

She opens the door opposite the living room door, and I see a glimpse of a small but neat kitchen before I head to the door she mentioned. I hear the tap run and I figure she's having a drink of water or something. I open her bedroom door and go inside.

It's very different to my room. While I hesitate to use the word messy, there is certainly a lot of clutter. I look around and confirm it's definitely not messy. It's her makeup and hair and skin products and all that kind of thing, but the fact they are all on display just looks like clutter to me.

Again, the room is very clean though and other than the messy dressing table, everything else is neat enough. Her bed is made nicely and beside it is a bedside cabinet with a book with a book mark sticking out of it. I glance down at the book title, expecting something romantic and girly. I grin at how wrong I am. She's reading the latest Stephen King book and judging by where her bookmark is, she's pretty far in.

I stop thinking about Louisa's partially read book or her cluttered dressing table when she walks into the room. She isn't messing about. She closes the door and as she walks towards me, she pulls her dress off over her head and throws it on the ground. Her bra and panties follow, and I take the hint and get up and take my t shirt off. Before I can start on my jeans, Louisa is there, and she undoes my button and my zipper and pushes the jeans down. I get my feet out of them when they fall down around my ankles and kick them away and then Louisa pushes me back down on the bed and gets on herself, straddling me. I scoot back a bit, and she follows and then she sits astride me, her already wet pussy on my rock hard cock.

She moves her hips a bit and my cock slides through her slit and I can't wait any longer. I grab her hips ready to flip her over, but she lifts herself slightly and reaches behind her body and takes hold of my cock. I let her do her thing as she lines it up with her opening and lowers herself back down onto me, impaling herself on my cock.

She takes my full length into her and moans and then she starts to move up and down on me. She moves slowly, teasing and tantalizing me. She is lovely and tight and every now and again, she tightens her pussy further, flexing the muscles there and enveloping me in an even tighter glove of warmth and wetness.

She glides up and down me and then she ups the pace, and I watch her, mesmerized, as her small breasts bounce up and down in time with her movements. She comes up and moves back down, but this time, instead of taking my full length, she concentrates her movements on the tip of my cock, using it to tease us both. I know I'm rubbing on her g spot by the way she bares down for a moment before she relaxes once more, and although I want to plunge all the way inside of her again, I must admit what she is doing feels good. There is no reprieve from the sensation of pleasure she is bringing to me as she moves faster again.

She throws her head back and I can see the tendons standing out in her neck as she comes hard. She is still doing her little up and down movement as she comes and I feel her pussy twitching around me and it is almost too much to take, but I hold myself back from coming. I don't want this to be over yet.

Louisa's head comes back up and she bites on her lower lip and smiles at me. Her face and chest are pink, and her eyes are wide, and she looks so damned delicious. I reach for her hips and take them in my hands and as I do, she pushes herself all of the way down, taking me fully inside of her again.

I'm unleashed and I keep a grip on her hips, using my hands to move her up and down on me. When I can't take it any longer, I push all of the way inside of her and hold her still on me and I come hard. I make an animalistic sounding growling noise as I come, and I see a shudder of pleasure go through Louisa as I do it. I spurt into her, enjoying the pleasure that shoots through my cock and balls and into my stomach and then I slip out of her.

She smiles down at me again and then she climbs off me and lays down beside me. I remain on my back and Louisa lays on her side facing me. I put my arm out and she rests her head on my shoulder, and I wrap my arm around her shoulders. She puts her hand flat on my stomach and traces a little circle shape with one finger nail.

We lay like that for a time, content and sated and getting our breaths back. I could happily lay here all night, but I know I have to respect Louisa's boundaries and if she doesn't want to spend the night with me, I won't force myself onto her.

"Do you want me to go?" I ask.

She shakes her head.

"No," she says, snuggling closer to me.

I'm confused now. I really thought she wanted to leave my place because she wasn't sure how she felt about us being together, but she seems happy enough for us to be together here. God does my apartment have some sort of smell or something like that? Something I haven't noticed that has given Louisa the ick? I feel as she's reading my thoughts as she speaks up without any further prompting from me.

"I didn't really want to leave your place, but I needed to come home and take my birth control pill," she says.

I relax and let out a soft laugh. So, she never wanted to get away from me then. Now I'm even more glad I didn't let her get a cab. I would have spent the whole night thinking she didn't want this when really, she just doesn't want to get pregnant the first time she sleeps with me.

"I think maybe you should keep it in your purse from now on," I say.

"Deal," Louisa agrees.

# CHAPTER
## Twenty~Three

**TIA**

I know I should end this thing with Luke before it goes any further. Nothing has changed with our situation since I kissed him. I'm still lying to him about my identity, and I still can't come clean yet about who I really am. The thing is, I don't want to end things between us. I want Luke so much physically and I know I'm definitely falling for him in more ways than just that way. Every time we kiss or fuck or even just hold each other, I can feel myself getting a little bit more attached to him, and I push my doubts further to the back of my mind to be dealt with later. What else can I do? I can't lose him, and I can't come clean, so that's the only option I really have left.

Yesterday at work, Luke sent for me to come to his office, and I thought for a moment I was in trouble, but he said he just wanted to see me. We kissed and he made me come with his fingers. It felt so naughty but so right at the same time and I have decided that I'm just going to focus on the feeling right part from now on. I will take each day as it comes and when I can tell Luke who I really am, then I will do it, and I will try and make him understand why I had to do this. And if he is so angry he doesn't want us to be together anymore then at least we will have had these seven weeks together.

Today is Saturday and Luke is picking me up soon. I'm not sure where we will be going – he just said he was going to show me the sights of Chicago. I almost slipped up when he asked where I wanted to go and I said I didn't know the city that well at all and that I wanted to see all of the major sights so he could choose one, but I quickly clarified that although I grew up in Chicago, I was mostly at school and then on the holidays, we would go off to other places. That's pretty much what Louisa did do, and she probably doesn't know Chicago's sights any better than I do. He didn't seem to think it was strange so I must have covered myself well enough.

Because I have no idea where we will be going, or what we will be doing, I have dressed in jeans, sneakers, and a checky shirt. I have made a bit of an effort with my hair and makeup so I look half decent, but I have settled on comfort for my outfit in case we have lots of walking to do. I don't want to be that high maintenance girl wobbling around in heels she can't really walk in.

Luke texts me to let me know he's leaving to pick me up, and I decide to go downstairs and wait for him. It's a warm enough day and it seems silly waiting for him to come up just for us both to leave straight away. I head for the door and grab my purse and check that I have everything I need. Wallet. Check. Cell phone. Check. Tissues. Check. Lip gloss. Check. Hair brush. Check. Oh, and my birth control pills. Check. I am good to go.

I take my keys from their hook by the door and choose a red belted coat to wear. I put the coat on and leave the apartment, locking the door behind me. I go downstairs and out of the main door and stand by the curb waiting for Luke. I don't have long to wait, and he pulls up beside me and I get into the car.

"Hi," I say.

Luke leans over and we kiss.

"Hi," he replies.

He pulls back away from the curb and out of my street and onto the main road.

"Ready to tell me where we're going?" I say.

"Well, I thought Lincoln Park Zoo, then lunch, and then The Shedd Aquarium for starters? How does that sound?" Luke says.

"Good," I reply. "Unless the aquarium treats the whales and such cruelly. I can't go somewhere where the poor things look depressed and lifeless."

"They don't," Luke says. "None of their animals are forced to perform, they eat a natural diet, and they get lots of attention from marine biologists. They have medical professionals on site and the only whales there are ones who wouldn't be able to survive in the wild. The place doesn't go hunting wild whales and poaching them."

"That sounds good then," I say. "You sound like you know a lot about the place."

"Conservation and animal protection are big passions of mine, and I donate a lot of money to the two places we will be visiting today because they both have the right ethos I believe," Luke says.

"That's sweet," I say. "I wish I could make a difference like that. I think the closest I'll come is being able to adopt a rescue dog once I have my career sorted and have a house rather than an apartment. I know that's not much though."

"It might not seem much to you. To the dog you adopt, it is everything," Luke says, and I smile. I like that way of thinking.

The drive isn't too long, and Luke pulls into the parking

lot of the Lincoln Park Zoo and finds a parking spot. We get out of the car and head towards the entrance. I'm shocked when I see the entrance fee is free.

"How come it's free?" I ask.

"They want to educate people about animals and their plights. Charging people rules out a lot of visitors," Luke explains.

He makes a good point, but I can't think of a single other zoo that employs the same strategy. This one must either be owned by someone mega rich who cares about the animals they house, or they do good fund raising events or something like that. Maybe local businesses sponsor them too. They must feed the animals and pay the staff somehow and they can't do all of that and all of the maintenance of the place without money.

We enter the zoo and hand in hand, we follow the trail painted on the ground. I can't help but shriek with delight when we come to a huge enclosure with a pride of lions inside. They are stretched out, relaxing, sleeping, just enjoying their day. The sight is so special, and I feel my eyes filling with tears as I watch the sleeping cats. Luke sees my reaction and squeezes my hand. I squeeze back.

"They're beautiful" I whisper, and Luke nods his head.

We move on and Luke and I chat as we go. Mostly, we talk about the animals we are seeing and the environments they are in, but we also talk a little bit about other things too. I feel like I'm really getting to know Luke and I hate that I have to be so vague in anything I tell him about myself or my family because he thinks I'm Louisa and that her family is my family. I can't tell him about how my mom worked her ass off to make sure I had everything I needed, or how we used to sit up late throughout December making Christmas decorations from colored cardboard and glitter because we couldn't afford to buy new ones. I guess I will have lots to tell him once my internship is over. Assuming he still wants to know me.

I stop myself from going down that path again and turn my focus instead to the animals again. We see all kinds of things: otters, flamingos, different kinds of birds and ducks, different kinds of monkeys, reptiles and insects. We see so much that I feel like I will never remember them all, but I love every minute of the trip, and I'm a little bit sad when it is over. I feel like I could happily spend weeks in here. I can come back whenever I want to though now that I know the place exists and it's not even like it will take a chunk of my salary to visit.

We decide to have our lunch in the little café within the zoo's grounds and at least give something back that way. We both order grilled cheese sandwiches with tomato soup, and I choose a can of orange soda and Luke chooses a can of grape soda. When our meals arrive, the soup is thick and tangy and the cheese is melty and stretchy, and I thoroughly enjoy my lunch.

"For something so simple, that was really good," Luke says.

"It was delicious," I agree.

"Would you like anything else?" Luke asks me.

"No thanks," I say.

Truthfully, the cakes and pastries look amazing, and I would love to try one, but we have the aquarium next, and I feel like if eat any more, I won't want to keep walking around. Luke goes and pays the bill, and we leave the café and then the zoo itself and go back to Luke's car. We get in and he drives to the aquarium. It's only a twenty minute drive and we are there. We get out of the car again and go to the entrance. This attraction isn't free, and I reach for my wallet.

"I'll pay for our tickets," I say.

"You'll do no such thing," Luke says.

"But …" I start.

Luke cuts me off before I get any further.

"I don't think you're a gold digger or any of that shit," he says. "I invited you here and I will be paying for it."

"But you got our lunch," I point out.

"And I'll be getting dinner too. And paying for whatever we do this evening," he says. "So, let's not make a scene."

I know when I'm beat, and I shrug one shoulder and Luke grins knowing he's won this time. He has won today, but I'll get him back another day. I now know I have to be more sneaky about it that's all.

Luke pays for our tickets, and we go inside. It's dark, although not so dark that we can't see to walk, the only light coming from dim blue bulbs that make it feel almost like we are under the sea ourselves. The air is filled with the sound of gushing water, little splashes, and children laughing and exclaiming at the sights. It is all under scored by the quiet hum of conversation.

We walk to the first tank, and I stand and peer inside. It's large and in the center is a red coral reef. All around it, fish of all colors and shapes and sizes swim around. Luke names a few of them for me and tells me a little bit about them. Watching the fish swim around is so relaxing and I could stand here all day, but I'm conscious that there are people behind us waiting to see the exhibition and that there is now a big gap in front of us where the people before us have moved on a while ago.

We move slowly to the next exhibition and while we are looking into the tank, Luke speaks up.

"About me wanting to pay for things," he says. "This is terribly vulgar to discuss, and it will make me sound like a massive dick, but it needs to be said. I grew up, not poor exactly, but not well off either. I know how hard it can be to juggle finances and try to afford days out as well as essentials. Now, I'm the CEO of a billion-dollar company and money is easy come, easy go to me. I know you're not in a position to throw money away if you are truly living on an intern's wage, and I really like you. I want to spoil you. Please let me do that."

I don't know what to say to that. It's a side to Luke I haven't considered, the side where he grew up pretty much like I did with essentials like food and clothes covered but treats and days out weren't common place.

"I currently earn more a day than you do in a month," Luke says.

Finally, I find myself nodding my agreement – if he earns that kind of money, I can live with him paying for me when we go places - and I look at Luke's reflection in the glass tank and see he is looking at mine.

"OK," I finally say.

He squeezes my hand, and we move on to the next tank.

"Dick mode deactivated," he says quietly as we walk, and I laugh and any remaining awkwardness from that conversation floats away on my laughter.

We look into the next few tanks and then we find ourselves outside and I can't help but squeal with joy as Luke leads me through a small, manned gate, and into what turns out to be the penguin enclosure. There is a walkway and lots of white marble flooring that I assume mimics ice, and there is a huge pool for them that goes beneath the walkways and, Luke tells me, a long way down.

Penguins waddle around doing their thing and they are the most adorable little things. They don't seem to fear humans although we are warned not to pet them or attempt to pick them up. We watch them for a few minutes and then the staff ushers us forward and out through another gate and we walk through a tunnel where we can see beneath the water and watch the penguins swim. They are much more graceful in the water than they are on land.

After the penguins, we go and watch the seals being fed. I can definitely see why people call seals sea dogs with their big, sad eyes and their cute little snouts. They eat the fishes thrown to them and then they frolic in the water and play. One of the staff does a talk about the seals, about where each one came from and why they are here, and I see what Luke meant. None of the seals here would survive in the wild and they are well cared for here, and letting people visit and see them not only supports their care financially; it also raises awareness of these beautiful creatures and some of the challenges they are facing as a species.

Next, we see sea otters and sea lions.

"Do they have a sea lion show?" I ask as we walk.

Luke shakes his head.

"No. There's no dolphin or whale shows either. If we time it right, we will see them being fed and we can listen to talks about them, but they stopped doing the shows," he says.

"Good," I reply.

As much as I wouldn't have been able to resist going to watch the shows, at the same time, it doesn't seem right to take any of these majestic creatures and have them perform for human entertainment. The dolphins are the next exhibit for us to look at and as they play and swim around, I find myself tearing up just from their sheer beauty. It's like watching small children play the way they are so energetic and innocent, and they do seem to like to show off to the people watching them, but this is so much nicer than an organized show, because it is the dolphins themselves choosing to do this.

After the dolphin enclosure, we go back inside and come to the largest exhibition yet. There are lots of creatures in the tank, but the main attraction is the pod of beluga whales that swim around in there. Again, I can feel myself tearing up just from looking at them. Luke tells me a bit about this particular pod and where they all came from. Five of the six where rescues that were found injured and were deemed unfit for rehabilitation back into the wild. They would have died without the aquarium taking over their care. The fifth one was born in the aquarium and although there was talk of releasing her, the mother's feelings were taken into account, and it was decided it would be too depressing for her to lose her baby and so she stayed. Having never known anything different, there is no reason to suspect she isn't completely happy, especially now that they are just left alone to live and not put through training and performances. She is with her family, and she is safe, and I think there isn't much more than that to a happy life.

We look at the whales for a long time, and then we head towards the last part of the aquarium, which is a long walk through a clear tunnel with the shark tank above and around it. There are several varieties of sharks and lots of other creatures in the huge tank, and walking through the tunnel, which is again bathed in a soft blue light, it really feels like I'm in the tank with them. It's an amazing experience and I'm trying to look in every direction at once to not miss anything.

I am a little bit sad when we come to the end of the tunnel because I was enjoying it so much, and when I look at my watch, I'm shocked to see that almost four hours have passed since we came here. Luke sees my expression and laughs.

"It doesn't feel like we've been here for that long at all does it?" he says, and I shake my head. I guess it wasn't just the sharks I enjoyed more than I realized.

We have finished the tour of the place though, and we leave and head back to Luke's car.

"I was thinking we could go to Navy Pier after the aquarium, but now I'm thinking that might be a bit much all in one day. The city has so much to see and do and I want to show you it all," he says. "But I want you to enjoy it and take it in, not just rush through it all."

"Well, we've got plenty of time to see it all. Show me more next weekend and the one after that and the one after that," I say. "I don't think I would appreciate another place properly now. I don't want the day to be over yet though either."

Luke purses up his lips and thinks for a moment.

"How about catching a movie? We can just sit and relax, and we don't have to go home yet," he says.

"That sounds like fun," I agree, and Luke starts his car engine and drives us to a nearby cinema.

We get there and go inside and spend a few moments deciding which film we want to watch. We settle on an action movie that I think we will both like and Luke gets us tickets and some popcorn to share and a soda each. We go into the movie theatre and take our seats. We have timed our entrance well, and the movie is just starting as we sit down. The theatre isn't very busy because it's that weird time where the afternoon crowd has drifted off and the nighttime crowd hasn't come out yet, so it's nice and quiet.

We eat and drink and watch the movie and when it's finished, we head out into the lobby and we both go to use our respective bathrooms and meet back in the lobby after-wards. We head back to Luke's car chatting about the movie and what we liked and disliked about it and we both agree that it was a bit far-fetched, but ultimately, a fun watch. It was definitely a good choice for where we are mentally where we wanted something fun, but not something where we had to concentrate too hard to follow it. Sometimes, an easy, far-fetched watch is just what is needed, and I feel like this was one of those times.

"Are you hungry?" Luke asks once we are in the car and ready to go. I nod. "Where do you fancy for dinner?"

"I'm not dressed to go to a nice restaurant," I say. "How about we get a pizza and eat it at my place?"

"You look perfectly fine," Luke says. "But a pizza does sound good though. Do you have a place near you that you use?"

I nod.

"Head back towards my building and I'll direct you from there," I say.

# CHAPTER
Twenty~Four

## LUKE

"I told you we should have gone for the medium size," Louisa laughs as she looks at the pizza box where half of our large pizza sits uneaten with both of us stuffed full already.

"You said you were starving. I believed you," I laugh. "It'll do for your breakfast tomorrow."

"Our breakfast," Louisa says shyly. "Assuming you're staying over."

"Assuming you want me to, then yes," I say, and Louisa nods her head again.

She gets up and closes the pizza box and takes it to the kitchen and then she comes back.

"I'm going to go jump in the shower. Make yourself at home," she says.

"Does that mean I can do whatever I want to do?" I say and Louisa nods her head. "Then I hope your shower is big enough for two."

She nods her head again and we both grin and then I'm

up and following her and we go to Louisa's bathroom where we both strip off. Her shower is an over bath one so there is plenty of room for us both in there. Louisa climbs into the bath tub first and switches the spray on, standing back with one hand in the stream of water while she waits for it to get warm. I push her forward and she shrieks as the cold water soaks her. She laughs and flicks some of the water at me and I get into the bath, and then she pulls me beneath the cold spray.

We're both laughing and trying to duck out of the stream of cold water, but it soon warms up and we relax and start to enjoy the water hitting our skin. After a few minutes, Louisa reaches for her shampoo. She opens the bottle, and I take it from her and squeeze a bit into my palm. I reach up and rub it into her hair and motion for her to turn around. She does so and I wash her hair and then I spend some time massaging her scalp. If her ohs and ahs are anything to go by, she likes the head massage, and I keep going as I rinse the soap back out of her hair. Next, I get her shower gel and put some of that on my hands and then I gently massage Louisa's whole body. I pay particular attention to her breasts and then to her clit, soaping her right up.

"You are a very dirty girl," I whisper in Louisa's ear as I continue to 'wash' her slit. "I have to make doubly sure that you are clean here."

She moans and leans back against me, and I keep running my fingers over her warm and slippery flesh until she goes rigid against me and her head lays back on my chest, her face contorted with pleasure.

When her orgasm finishes, I pull my fingers away from her slit and I start rinsing her down. She lets me rinse her clean and then she turns around and gives me a naughty looking smile.

"Your turn," she says, and she gets the shower gel and

returns the favor of washing my body. Her touch lingers on my inner thighs and my already hard cock hardens further.

Louisa gets some more shower gel and then she starts to work my cock with both of her hands. She moves them up and down and she also twists them from side to side, her two hands working in opposite directions. Her grip is light enough so as not to leave a friction burn, but firm enough to feel amazing. It's like nothing I have ever felt before and I know if she keeps on doing that, I'm going to come and I don't want to come in her shower, I want to come in her.

With a sense of regret despite it being what I want to do, I pull her hands away from my cock and kiss her deeply and then I turn her around and she spreads her legs and bends over, her hands resting on the wall. I push inside of her. She's warm and wet, and the shower gel and the water make her even more slippery than usual, and I glide in and out of her like we were made to fit together like this.

She moves with me, pushing herself off her hands and back onto me so I go deeper into her and then we move and writhe and moan and finally, after a few excruciatingly intense moments, we come together with each other's names on our lips. Louisa straightens up and turns around and we wrap our arms around each other and stand beneath the spray of water that way until we get our breaths back. Finally, we break apart and then we finish up in the shower and get out, each of us wrapping ourselves in one of Louisa's large, fluffy towels. We go through to her bedroom where I sit on the bed and watch her as she blow dries her hair.

When her hair is dry, she brushes it through and then she opens a drawer inside of her wardrobe and pulls out a pair of short shorts and a vest top. She drops her towel to the ground, and I watch as she pulls on the shorts and the vest top and comes over and gets under her comforter.

"Do you want to watch a movie in bed?" she asks.

"No," I say. I grin at her. "But what I do want to do involves you in the bed, just without the clothes."

Louisa laughs and when I stand up and drop the towel, she pulls the comforter back and invites me into her bed beside her.

# CHAPTER
## Twenty~Five

**TIA**

Yesterday was the best day ever. Luke and I visited some fantastic places, and the company was obviously good and spending a full day and night together like that and not getting even remotely sick of each other's company tells me that Luke and I definitely have something special between us. To be honest, I'm kind of missing his presence already and he's only been gone for like an hour or so.

We woke up this morning and Luke told me to stay where I was. He got out of bed and came back with our half eaten pizza and some orange juice for each of us. We ate the rest of the pizza for breakfast in bed and then we made love. Afterwards, Luke said he had to go because he was having brunch with his mom. For a horrible minute, I had thought he was going to invite me along. I don't have any issues with meeting Luke's family per se. As I said, I think we have something special and for all I would normally say it's far too soon, it doesn't feel that way for us. But I really don't want to have to meet Luke's family as Louisa. It's bad enough that I have to lie to him, but I think – I hope – that when the time comes, I can make him understand why I had to do this, but I don't think I could ever make his family understand and I would really rather wait to meet them, but I couldn't think of a good reason not to go if Luke had asked me. I didn't want to have to tell him it was too soon, because it's not how I feel at all.

We are seeing each other again tonight – he said I have to choose what we do because he chose everything yesterday. I'm debating some options when my cell phone rings. I expect it to be Luke, but when I pick it up and look at the screen, it says it's Justin calling. I press answer and bring my cell phone up to my head.

"Hi," I say.

"Hey you," Justin says. "How are you?"

"I'm good," I say. "How about you?"

"Same, same," Justin says. "Listen Tia, I've met someone. A girl. We haven't been seeing each other that long, but I really like her, and I think she might even be the one. Would it be weird if I asked you to have dinner with us tonight and meet her?"

I think for a moment. That would solve my problem of what Luke and I can do tonight and it might be nice to meet this girl – she and I could even become friends.

"It's not weird at all," I say. "I'd love to meet her. And actually, I'm seeing someone too. We should make it a double date."

"That works," Justin says. "What about The Pasta Bowl? I'll book us a table for eight o'clock."

"Yeah, that sounds good," I say. "I've never been to the restaurant though."

"The food is lovely. Obviously Italian. You'll like it," he says.

"Tell me about your girl then," I say.

"Her name is Emily, she's twenty-three and she's a teaching assistant in a high school," Justin says. "She's really pretty and she's funny and we seem to have a lot in common."

"That's good. She sounds like a good match for you," I say.

"She is," Justin says. "What about your new guy?"

"His name is Luke and he's my boss," I say. "So, get all of your ick at that situation out now."

"Hey, no judgement here. As long as you like him and he treats you right, that's all that matters," Justin says, and I smile and nod even though he can't see me.

"He treats me like a princess," I say. "Something happened at work, and I had to pretend I had diarrhea – I know, don't ask – anyway, even after that, he still wanted to date me. I reckon that makes him a keeper."

"It definitely does," Justin agrees laughing.

"Oh, that reminds me. You'll have to call me Louisa tonight," I say. "Do you think you can do that without slipping up?"

"Sure," Justin says. "But do you really think it's a good idea to lie to this guy like that if you're that into him?"

"Probably not," I admit. "But I don't really have a choice now and it's only for a few more weeks."

"Ok, well see you at eight o'clock then, Louisa," Justin says, emphasising the name.

I say goodbye and end the call, and then I text Luke and tell him what I have chosen for us to do for the evening and checking he is ok with us going on a double date. He texts back confirming that's fine and that he would like to get to know a friend of mine.

I wish I could introduce him to Louisa. More than that, I wish I could tell Louisa about him. I could go into a ton of detail with her that I just wouldn't feel comfortable discussing with Justin, and I know she would be so excited for me. But I can't tell her. Not yet. Not when I'm meant to be her. She might be ok with it, but she might be really mad at me, and I know I should have checked with her before I let anything happen between Luke and me, but I was determined I wasn't going to let anything happen and by the time it did, it was too late to check in.

I hope when my internship is over, Luke and I can laugh about the name thing one day, and I hope Louisa and I can do the same thing. Until then, I have to keep Louisa and Luke apart, but there's definitely no harm in him meeting Justin.

# CHAPTER
## Twenty-Six

### LUKE

Although I'm happy to be meeting a friend of Louisa's because I take it must mean that she thinks we are going to last, I must admit I was kind of hoping we would spend the evening just the two of us. Having said that, Justin and Emily are both nice people and the four of us have been getting on really well and having a good laugh together, and I can't say I'm not enjoying the night.

"To good company and good food," Justin says, raising his glass.

Me, Louisa, and Emily all raise our glasses and repeat the toast, clinking our glasses together and drinking. The food has been really good too, he is right about that. I haven't been here for years, but I think it might become somewhere I come more often. It could even be somewhere I would bring potential advertisers for a working lunch if it's open lunch times. I will have to check the website tomorrow.

We still have dessert to go, and I'm already full, but I have no intention of missing out on the cannoli I've ordered.

"Please excuse me," Emily says, pushing her chair back. "I have to use the ladies' room."

"I'll come with you," Louisa says and the two of them leave the table together.

I watch Louisa as she walks away, and I glance quickly at Justin and see him watching Emily. It seems those girls have both of us wrapped around their little fingers and if Emily is even a little bit like Louisa, she doesn't even know it.

"You know you're not good enough for her, don't you?" Justin says when the women are out of sight.

"Excuse me?" I say, keeping my voice level because although he has pissed me off, I don't want to show it at the moment because I'm sure I must have misheard him.

"I said you're not good enough for her," Justin says. "She should be with me."

"What about Emily?" I say, purposely not commenting on Louisa because I'm afraid that I will punch his face in if I do and I really don't want to do that in the middle of a restaurant.

"Emily's a cool girl," Justin says. "But she's no Louisa."

On that one, we agree, but I don't say that.

"Well, you'd best get used to being with Emily because Louisa is mine," I say.

"You're just keeping her warm for me mate," Justin says with a grin. "We were together before, and we will end up back with each other. You're just a wild oat that needed to be sowed first."

"You're delusional," I say. "And if you lay so much as a finger on her, I won't hesitate to knock you out."

I'm sure Justin would have had some sarcastic come back to that, but he has to keep it in because the ladies are back, and he doesn't have the balls to say it in front of them. I do, but I choose to let it go because I don't want to embarrass Emily, although I do wonder if I should warn her. I decide not to. I don't know her and their relationship is none of my business.

Our desserts arrive as the women are sitting back down and we all focus mostly on them, eating quietly except for the odd comment about how good the dishes are. Louisa tops everyone's glasses up from the shared bottle of wine on our table and uses up the last of it. I'm glad because I'm ready to get out of here the second, I can do so without looking rude.

"Anyone want coffees?" Justin asks. I shake my head and so does Emily. Louisa doesn't seem to have heard him. "Tia? Coffee?"

Louisa looks up then and glares at him.

"Shit, sorry," Justin says. "Tia was an old nickname I had for Louisa when we were dating. She had this phase where all she drank was Tia Maria and the name just stuck."

I raise an eyebrow at Louisa who just looks down at the table and refuses to meet my eye. Emily looks about ready to punch Justin, and I guess I'm not the only one who didn't know before tonight that these two used to date.

"No one for coffee. Ok. I'm going to go and grab us a round of Sambuca shots instead then," Justin says. "That's much more fun anyway isn't it."

He seems awkward and embarrassed, and I think the shots are just an excuse to leave the table, which he does, so quickly, he almost knocks his chair over as he gets up, but he catches it at the last second.

"I'll come and help you carry them," Emily says, and she gets up a bit more calmly than Justin and the two of them go towards the bar.

"When were you planning on telling me that Justin is your ex-boyfriend?" I ask when Louisa and I are alone.

She finally looks at me.

"Truthfully? I wasn't planning on telling you at all. It's ancient history, we weren't good together as a couple, and we are just friends now," she says. "It's not something I really think of so it's not something that would have come up."

I figure if Louisa was still into Justin, she wouldn't have chosen to introduce me to him, but I'm still kind of angry that she hid that from me. Especially in light of what he said to me while the women were away from the table.

"He's still into you," I say.

"No, he isn't," Louisa says. I go to interrupt her, but she goes on, ignoring my attempt to butt in. "And even if he is, it doesn't matter because I am not into him. I am into you."

Most of the anger goes out of me at that. How can I be angry at her for not telling me something that she doesn't deem important, and her not deeming it important is actually a point in my favor too. I'm still angry at Justin, but he's not important to me and I decide to just let it go. He can be as bitter and as crude as he likes. I've still got the girl.

I glance up to see if he and Emily have been served yet and see the bar is empty. I look around and see them beside the bar in a quiet corner of the restaurant. It looks like they are arguing, because their arms are gesticulating wildly and Emily, who is facing towards us, looks absolutely fuming. I nod subtly towards the arguing couple.

"It looks like Emily isn't taking the news too well," I say.

"Hopefully she will get over it, because Justin actually said to me earlier that he thinks she's the one," Louisa says.

I have to hand it to Justin; he is good. He's letting Louisa believe that he only wants friendship too, that he has moved on and found this amazing girl, and the whole time, he is just biding his time, waiting to get her on the hook again. I'm not stupid enough to voice this thought to Louisa.

"Oh no, she's storming off," Louisa says.

I look back up in time to see Emily reaching the door and leaving the restaurant. Justin doesn't go after her. Instead, he heads back to the bar and picks the drinks he must have already purchased up, and he comes back towards the table with the four shots in his hands. He sits down and seems to deflate as he does so.

"I was going to say Emily had a family emergency and had to leave, but what's the point in lying? She has ended things with me and left," he says. He flashes a grin at Louisa. "I guess she feels she can't live up to you."

"Should I go after her?" Louisa says. "Tell her how things are with us, that she has literally nothing to worry about?"

Justin looks even more deflated as he shakes his head.

"No, let her go. If she's going to throw a tantrum whenever she doesn't like something, I'm better off without her," Justin says.

"It was hardly a tantrum," I interject. "She just lost trust in you because you lied to her, that's all."

"Luke," Louisa says. "Do you have to be so blunt? Justin is upset."

"Sorry," I say. "I didn't mean it to come out like that."

I'm not sorry in the least and I definitely meant it to come out like that. The only reason I toned down what I said was because I didn't want Louisa to think I was having a sly dig at her because she hadn't told me about Justin.

Justin pushes a shot towards me and one towards Louisa. He picks up the other two.

"To being single and getting an extra shot," he says, and he downs the two shots one after the other.

I shrug and swallow mine and Louisa does the same, grimacing at the taste as she swallows it.

"Maybe we should call it a night then," I say.

Louisa nods her agreement, but Justin shakes his head.

"Don't go yet Louisa, please," he says. "I really don't want to be alone at the minute."

Louisa looks at me begging me with her eyes to understand.

"Do you mind?" she says to me. "You can go if you want to, and I'll get a cab later."

"Don't be silly," I say. "We can stay a while."

Like I'm leaving her alone with someone who has already made it clear he wants her back and now he's doing the whole sad puppy thing to get her attention. As much as I don't really want to spend any more time with this loser, I will sit here and pretend to be all sympathetic and that will hopefully be the last of Justin I have to see.

# CHAPTER
## Twenty-Seven

**TIA**

Am I supposed to be pissed off with Luke, because he made it clear he wants to leave, but then he also made it clear he's not comfortable to leave me alone with Justin? I'm meant to be annoyed with him, yes. But confession time. I'm not. I actually think it's kind of hot that he's a bit jealous about me. I'm not going to play on that or anything – I'm not one of those toxic girls who flirt with other guys to try to make their man jealous – but it's still nice when it happens naturally.

"I'll go get us some drinks," Luke says. "Gin and tonic, Louisa?" I nod. "Justin? What are you drinking?"

"Jack Daniels and coke please," he says.

Luke gets up and leaves the table.

"Give her time to calm down and then call her and apologize," I say to Justin. "She'll come round and see it's not that big of a deal."

"That's it though, isn't it? It's not a big deal and I don't think I've done anything I need to apologize for. She says I've lied to her, but I haven't. If she had asked me if we had dated, I would have said yes. She never asked and I just didn't think to mention it," he says.

"You could try explaining that to her, but if you really like her and want her back, trust me, the apology is the quickest way to do it," I say.

Luke arrives back at the table before Justin can say anymore. He's empty handed, and he doesn't sit down.

"I've taken care of the bill and ordered our drinks to drink in the bar area. I thought it might be better than staying in the dining area and taking up a table," he says.

"You didn't have to pay the bill," Justin says. "I can afford a meal out you know."

"I don't doubt it," Luke says. "But never the less, it's covered. Let's go."

"I prefer it here," Justin says.

Both of them look at me. Oh great. Just what I need. I don't want to have to take sides between my friend and my man and I decide instead to choose where I would rather be. I stand up.

"Come on Justin," I say. "The wait staff needs to turn tables over to make their wages, you know that."

Justin waited tables in college, and I know he knows this, and once I remind him of it, he nods sheepishly and gets up and the three of us move through to the bar. The bar area is much more intimate than the restaurant with booths with red velvet seating and the majority of the light coming from candles on the tables. It's much more relaxing and the seating is every bit as comfortable as it looks.

I slip in on one side of the booth and Justin goes to get in beside me, but Luke subtly blocks his path, and Justin ends up sitting opposite me. Luke gives the bartender a wave and sits down beside me.

The bartender brings the drinks over and telling him who

has what drink is the first words any of us have spoken since we sat down. I don't like the atmosphere brewing between Justin and Luke and so I search my mind for something I know they both like and the answer is immediately obvious – animals. Luke donates to several animal conservation charities and Justin volunteers at a local shelter. Surely that's some common ground.

"Luke is quite involved in animal conservation," I say to Justin and then to Luke, "Justin volunteers at a local shelter."

It seems to do the trick as the two men look at each other in a new light and then they start asking each other questions about what exactly they do, and they discuss how sad yet rewarding the shelter is. The conversation flows easily now, although for the most part, I'm not involved. I like animals and of course I don't want to see them hurt, but I don't really know enough about what they're talking about to bring anything to the conversation and so I don't try to. To be honest, I'm content to sip my drink and listen to them talking. I love it when Luke talks about something he's passionate about; he really comes to life.

"Any new projects on the horizon?" Justin asks Luke.

"There's a seal been brought to the nearby animal hospital. It looks like it's been attacked by a shark apparently. One of its flippers has been bitten almost all of the way off. It can still swim, but not fast enough to avoid predators or catch food. If it was released, it would die. They were going to euthanize it, but the Shedd agreed that he would be welcome to live with their other seals and he wouldn't be in danger and could live perfectly happily. Because it could never be rehabilitated to the wild, the animal hospital didn't feel like it could spend resources on it, so I paid for its care," Luke says. "I wish I could do more than just throw money at situations, but I genuinely don't have the time to volunteer in person. I wish I did. People like you are the ones who make the most difference."

Justin shakes his head.

"Not at all," he says. "I love volunteering and spending time with the animals, but without benefactors such as you, the shelter wouldn't even exist."

They go back and forth with this and suddenly they aren't competing to see who is the most alpha, they are each trying to say the other person does something better than they do. In the end, I can't stand it anymore and I speak up.

"Can we just agree what you both do is important and on behalf of creatures everywhere, I thank you," I say.

"Sorry," Luke says with a grin. "We got a bit carried away there didn't we?"

"You think?" I tease him.

"You should come by the shelter one day," Justin says. "Bring Louisa. It'll be nice to see you both and maybe those big pockets can extend to help the shelter a bit when you see the place."

"Sure, I'm up for that," Luke says, and I nod my agreement too, glad that they have found some common ground and seem to be getting along. The conversation also seems to have taken Justin's mind off Emily too.

We order another round of drinks and now Luke and Justin have moved on to talking about other things and some of the stuff, I join in with. I can still sense a bit of an underlaying atmosphere between the two men, but for the most part, they seem to be getting along quite well, and even I'm surprised at how much they actually have in common.

"Same again?" Justin says when we finish the round.

I shake my head.

"Not for me thank you. I have work tomorrow and I want a clear head. In fact, I think it's probably time I called it a night," I say.

"It's barely ten o'clock," Justin says.

"I know. But like I said, I have work tomorrow," I repeat. "I'll make it up to you I promise."

He looks ready to argue the fact, but Luke stands up and starts to put his jacket on and I follow his lead.

"Can we drop you anywhere?" Luke asks Justin.

"No, it's ok, I'm not far from here. I'll just walk," he says. "I might call Emily on the way."

We head out of the building and Luke and I are going to be heading for the parking lot and Justin is going the other way so we say our goodbyes. Justin and I hug and Luke shakes Justin's hand.

"We have to grab lunch one day," Justin says to me, and I nod.

"Of course," I say. "Text me later in the week and we'll arrange something."

He nods his agreement, and something comes to me.

"Oh, wait," I say. "You two should exchange numbers and meet up one evening for drinks or whatever and discuss your animal stuff further."

I can see both men trying to think of a reason to not exchange numbers, but it seems neither of them can come up with anything and so they do the exchange while I look on approvingly. If they spend a bit more time together, I think Luke will see that Justin is a good guy and stop worrying about supposedly him liking me as more than just a friend.

I feel like they've only really exchanged

numbers to appease me, and I will probably have to push Luke to reach out to Justin, but I really want them to get along. I only have two real friends here and Justin is one of them, and I can't introduce Luke to the other one yet, so it really is quite important to me.

# CHAPTER
## Twenty~Eight

## LUKE

My cell phone pings and my top desk drawer rattles with the vibration. I open the drawer and take the cell phone out and see I have an unread text message. I smile, expecting it to be from Louisa. I open the message and my smile fades because the text message isn't from Louisa or anyone I would want to hear from really. It's from Justin and he's asking me if I want to go for a drink with him tonight.

My first instinct is to text back and just say no but I know Louisa wants Justin and me to get along and I don't want to be the one who seems to be getting in the way of that. Plus, I know Justin doesn't like me anymore than I like him, and I am curious as to why he's extended this invitation. I guess it's so he looks like the good guy in front of Louisa for reaching out first and if I say no, it's even more brownie points for him.

Tonight is actually a good night for me to go out with him. Last week, Louisa joined a book club because she wants to get to know more people in the city and she enjoys reading so it seemed like a good fit. The host for this week had to cancel and Louisa offered to host the meeting at her place and it's tonight.

Fuck it, I think to myself, and I text Justin back.

"Sure. Anywhere in particular?" I send.

Justin texts back the name of a pub I've never heard of, and I Google it. It's not that far from my place and it's as good a place as any other to go to, I guess. I text him back agreeing and saying I will be there around seven thirty to which I get a thumbs up emoji back.

I put my cell phone away and again, I can't help but wonder what Justin is up to here. I'm sure it's the brownie points with Louisa thing, but I can't help but think there is more to it than that and I don't know why I feel this way or what it might be. I'm not particularly nervous. Justin doesn't scare me, and I know if it came to it, I could take him in a fight, but I am intrigued.

Not long after the text exchange, Louisa appears in my office with a message from Karl about what the app the team is working on. I give her a reply for Karl, and she thanks me and goes to leave.

"Before you go," I say, and she turns back to face me. "Justin texted me earlier to ask me to have a drink with him tonight."

"Did you say yes?" she asks, and I nod.

"Good," she says. "I'd really like you two to be friends."

Don't push it, I think to myself.

"Me too," I say out loud.

It's a lie, but it's a harmless enough lie and I don't feel bad telling it, because I'm willing to see Justin socially if it makes Louisa happy.

∾

I arrive at the pub Justin named, and I go inside. It's pretty quiet and I look around and I don't see Justin. Couples occupy a few of the booths and a few small groups sit around some of the tables. The jukebox is playing something I vaguely recognize but couldn't name.

I head to the bar and order a bottle of Coors. It comes ice cold and refreshing and I pay for the drink and take a table where I can see the door and Justin will be able to see me when he comes in. He's late, but only a minute or two and I decide to let it go, even when he sits down without an apology for being late.

"How are you?" I ask, determined to be polite to him.

"Pretty good," he says. "You?"

"Yeah, I'm ok," I say. "Did you manage to sort things out with Emily?"

Justin shakes his head.

"To be honest, despite what I said to Louisa, I didn't feel comfortable apologizing to Emily when I hadn't actually done anything wrong. It felt like I was setting myself up to fail, you know what I mean?" he says.

I nod. I don't particularly want to agree with him over Louisa, but I do get what he's saying, and I don't really think anyone should apologize just because they think it's what the other person wants to hear. It has to be from a genuine place. And also, I think he's right about not apologizing if the person doesn't think they are in the wrong, because then, if Emily is a bit of a bitch, she will expect Justin to back down and apologize to her for nothing every time they have an argument.

We talk about Emily a bit more and then we move on to last night's game. It's a safe topic, but I can feel myself warming slightly to Justin. He seems like an ok guy really, and I can't exactly blame him for being pissed off at losing Louisa – I would be too. He doesn't seem to have an ulterior motive for inviting me out for a drink and as the night goes on, we talk about all kinds of things from work to politics to travelling and everything in between.

It's getting towards the end of the night, and I feel a bit tipsy and judging by the slight slur in Justin's words, I think he likely feels the same way.

"You know, you're actually a good guy," Justin says. High praise indeed. "In other circumstances, I really think we could be friends, don't you?"

"What do you mean, in other circumstances?" I ask him.

"Well, you're not going to want to be friends with me once I take Louisa back away from you, are you?" he says.

I shrug my shoulders.

"I have no idea because it's not going to happen. I probably don't want to be friends with someone who would even try such a thing though, so I guess you're right," I say.

"I don't understand you man," Justin says.

I don't want to give him the satisfaction of asking him why, but I am curious and although I feel like I should just leave, something keeps me sitting here.

"Why not?" I ask.

"Well, you know Louisa was with me first. And you know I am going to get her back. Why are you standing in the way of this? Why don't you just be a real man and step aside and let us be happy?" Justin says.

I realize in that moment that Justin is ever so slightly unhinged. He genuinely seems to believe that him and Louisa are the end game and that I'm just a bump in the road to their happily ever after. I don't have the want or the energy to argue with someone who thinks the way Justin does, and so I pick my bottle up, drain my drink and stand up.

"Stay away from Louisa," I say.

I head for the door, and I hear scuffling behind me as Justin gets up and follows me out of the pub. I'm getting angry now and he's going to be sorry if he pushes me too far here. I was planning to call a cab and wait here for it to come, but I really don't want to wait with Justin, and I hope if I walk away, he will go his own way.

It doesn't work though. I walk in the direction of my place, knowing Justin's place is in the opposite direction. I hear the pub door open and close, and Justin follows behind me. I'm not even to the next building yet and I don't want this creep following me any further. I stop walking and turn around.

"Seriously. Why don't you just fuck off?" I snap.

"Why don't you take your own advice?" Justin says. "Fuck off away from Louisa or I will make you sorry."

"Is that so?" I say with a raised eyebrow.

"Damned right it is," Justin says.

He slurs something else I can't make out, and then he's coming at me. I reach out to shove him, shocked he's taken things this far. What a fucking loser he is. I can't believe I thought he was an ok guy, even for a moment.

# CHAPTER
## Twenty~Nine

## TIA

I had a really good time this evening with the people from the book club. We talked about the book we've just finished, Blindness by Jose Saramago, and afterwards, we just chatted in general. We drank wine and ate the snacks I had prepared, and I definitely think the night was a success. I'm already looking forward to our next meeting when we will discuss our next book, The Turn of the Screw by Henry James.

The meeting went later than I thought it would and it's now almost eleven o'clock and I've just finished washing the dishes and tidying up after the last guests left. I'm tired, but pleasantly so, the sort of tired you feel after a good meal or a fun time.

I'm debating between whether to shower now and have an extra fifteen minutes in bed in the morning, or whether to just crash now and shower in the morning. I'm still debating it when my intercom buzzes.

At first, I think one of the book club group members must

have left something behind, but I can't see anything that doesn't belong, and I can't see anyone coming back at this time of night for something left behind anyway. I smile when I realize it's most likely Luke finished his drinks with Justin and decided to pop in. I go over to the intercom and press the talk button.

"Hi," I say.

"Hi Tia. Can I come up?" a voice says.

It's not Luke and it takes me a second to place the voice. Justin. He's obviously alone because he called me Tia not Louisa. He sounds a bit tipsy, and I don't particularly want to let him in drunk at this time of the night.

"I'm just about to go to bed," I say.

"Please Tee, it's important," he says.

"Five minutes," I relent with a sigh I hope Justin doesn't hear.

I press the button to unlock the door and when I hear it open, I release the button. I go to my apartment door and unlock it and open it. I go back to the living room to wait for Justin to appear.

I don't have to wait long. I hear my front door close and then he's in the living room doorway and my jaw drops when I see him. Both of his eyes are black and swollen. His nose looks slightly crooked, and blood slowly trickles from it, although judging by the front of his shirt, it was gushing out a lot faster than that when it first happened. He has a small cut above one eyebrow and his bottom lip is cut and swollen.

"What the fucking hell happened to you?" I say.

He waves my question away with the flick of one hand and then he winces at the movement.

"It doesn't matter. I just came to see if you have any painkillers. I know I don't have any in," he says.

"Go and sit down at the dining table," I say, pointing to

the door to the kitchen and dining room in one. "While I go and have a look for some painkillers, gauze and steri-strips."

Justin does as I say, and I go to the bathroom. I open my bathroom cabinet and pull out a bottle of painkillers and some gauze and a packet of steri-strips. I go to the kitchen and run the tap and fill a glass with water. I take the glass and two of the painkillers to Justin. He takes them and thanks me. While he's swallowing the painkillers, I go back to the sink, and I fill a bowl with warm water. I go to the table and sit down beside Justin. He sees the bowl and the gauze and shakes his head.

"You don't have to do any of that," he says.

"Shush," I tell him.

He tries to smile but winces instead.

I start with the cut above his eyebrow first because out of all of his injuries, it looks the least painful and the easiest to deal with. I dab it gently with wet gauze and see it's barely more than a deep scratch when the dried blood washes away.

I go to his nose next and begin to clean all of the dried blood off his top lip and chin. He keeps sucking breath in between his teeth when presumably I hurt him, but he doesn't moan or pull away and I try to get on with it quickly to get it over with for him.

I dab at the cut on his bottom lip next. This one is pretty deep, and I get up and get a pair of kitchen scissors. I cut the steri-strips into small strips, and I hold the wound together and stick the strips over it to keep it closed. When I'm done, Justin looks a fair bit better, but it's still clear to see he has taken one hell of a beating.

"What happened to you?" I ask again.

He just shakes his head.

"Where was Luke when this happened?" I say, trying another tactic.

Justin just looks down at the table and refuses to look at

me. It makes me wonder what state Luke is in and if Justin got him into some sort of fight and doesn't want to have to admit it to me.

"Look I'm obviously going to find out," I say. "If you don't tell me, I'm going to call Luke."

"No, don't do that," Justin says, looking up finally.

"Then you tell me what happened," I say.

He's quiet long enough that I don't think he's going to tell me, but then he starts to speak and I kind of wish he hadn't told me.

"Luke did it," he says.

I have to have misheard him, surely. Or misunderstood him. Yes, that must be it. Maybe it was Luke who got Justin into a fight. That doesn't seem likely either, but it must be what he means.

"Did what?" I say.

"This," he says, pointing to his face.

"What? No," I say shaking my head. "Luke wouldn't do that."

He wouldn't. Not Luke. He's not the sort of guy to be getting drunk and fighting.

"Why would he do that?" I ask.

"Because he's jealous. Because he knows I still want you and I think he knows deep down that you still want me too," Justin says.

I want to believe Luke couldn't be capable of doing such a thing to someone I consider a friend, but I have seen his jealous side once or twice myself and while he has kept it under control, maybe this time, he just saw red. If Justin said to him what he just said to me, I could see Luke being almighty fucking pissed off. But to do this?

It doesn't make sense to me that Luke would go this far, even if Justin wound him up. But at the same time, Justin was out with Luke and clearly someone has done this to him.

"Please don't talk like that Justin," I say. "We've been over this, and we both have agreed we're better as friends."

"I know. I'm sorry," he says. "I worded that badly. I just think Luke thinks that's what's going on."

I've done nothing to make Luke think that I want anyone else but him. I know I haven't. But I have to wonder what lies Justin has been feeding him. Nothing is going to be resolved until I speak to Luke, and as much as I want to speak to him now, I don't want this to be a conversation we have over the phone. I want to be able to see Luke when I confront him so that I can see his expression.

"I'll call you a cab," I say to Justin. "And I will talk to Luke about this tomorrow."

"Thanks," Justin says.

I go and get my cell phone from the living room and quickly call Justin a cab. I go back to the kitchen and tell him it's on its way. He stands up.

"Thank you, Tee," he says. "For sorting this out."

He points to his face as he says it.

"Of course," I say. "I would tell you to go to the hospital with your nose, but I know you won't."

"I'll be ok," he says.

"At least take these," I say, holding out the bottle of painkillers to him.

He takes them and puts them in his pocket and thanks me again. He starts towards the door, and I follow him out. He opens my front door and moves into the corridor.

"I hate to say this, but I really think you should break up with Luke," he says. "You've seen now what he's capable of. What if next time he gets annoyed or jealous, it's at you?"

"Good night, Justin," I say, not wanting to go into that with him.

"Good night," he says, accepting my decision to not discuss it.

He walks away and I gently close and lock the door. I turn around and lean back against it. I sigh and shake my head. I don't know what has happened tonight, but I will get to the bottom of it, and I will decide from there what happens with Luke and me. He at least deserves a chance to explain his side of the story, and no matter how angry he happened to get, I don't for a second believe he would hurt me.

# CHAPTER
## Thirty

### LUKE

I look up from my desk, shocked when my office door opens. No one knocked and everyone knows to knock. Besides that, I didn't even know anyone else was at work yet. It's only just gone half past eight and mostly, people come in for nine. My shock and slight annoyance at the fact that my visitor didn't knock on my office door fades away when I see Louisa coming in. I open my mouth to say good morning to her, but something in her expression stops me and I frown instead.

"Are you ok?" I say, standing up.

She nods her head and closes my door.

"Sit down please," she says. "I need to talk to you. It's not about work which is why I'm here outside of work time."

I sit down and she sits down opposite me.

"Did you beat the crap out of Justin last night?" she says.

I'm not sure what I was expecting, but it certainly wasn't that. What the hell has made her think that?

"Of course not," I say. "Why would you even think that?"

"Because Justin said you did," Louisa says.

"Oh, and Justin is the picture of honesty, is he? If Justin said it, it must be true," I snap.

"There's no need to be like that about it," Louisa says. "Justin turned up at my place last night and he had been beaten badly. And he said you did it. I don't want to believe it's true, but I had to ask."

"Justin is a fucking liar," I say. "I didn't beat him, but given the trouble he has stirred up, I'm not going to lie. I kind of wish I had."

"That's an awful thing to say," Louisa replies. "His face was a mess."

I shrug my shoulders, and she shakes her head at me. I'm not going to pretend I'm too upset at Justin getting the smack he deserves, especially not when he used the experience to try and cause trouble between Louisa and me.

"What did happen then?" she asks.

"I have no idea," I say. "But if I had to guess, I would say he started running his mouth to the wrong person. We were having a perfectly pleasant evening and then I think he got a bit too drunk, and he started saying he had you first and he was going to get you back and I should just step aside. I was annoyed, but I didn't want to cause a scene, so I got up and left the pub and I thought that would be the end of it. But of course, it wasn't, because Justin followed me outside and continued to taunt me. I shoved him away from me when he came at me and that was it. I left then and he stayed put. Obviously, something happened after I had left but I don't know what."

"OK," Louisa says. She looks less angry and more confused now. "I'm sorry, but I had to ask you. You understand that don't you?"

I'm pissed off that she felt like she needed to ask me actually, but at the same time, I can see it from her point of view, and I guess if the roles were reversed, I would have asked her what happened. I nod.

"I believe you, but I just can't see why Justin would lie. Do you think maybe he got jumped from behind and he thought it was you?" Louisa says.

I shake my head.

"He lied because he's fucking toxic. Why can't you see that?" I shout.

I didn't mean to shout at her, but I can't help it. I do get why she asked, but I also get the impression she only half believes me, and she's still looking for excuses for Justin's lies. I can feel my anger rising to the surface and if Justin was here now, I think I would punch the bastard.

# CHAPTER
## Thirty-One

TIA

"He's my friend," I snap back at Luke when he asks me why I can't see that Justin is toxic. He isn't toxic, as I said, he's my friend, and I really hate the way Luke is constantly judging him. Something obviously happened last night, and Justin obviously thinks Luke was involved somehow, and even if he wasn't, that doesn't mean Justin isn't just genuinely mistaken.

"Oh, open your fucking eyes. He's not your friend. He is hanging around hoping you decide to get back with him," Luke shouts.

He doesn't wait for an answer although I'm already shaking my head when Luke stands up. I really want to believe Luke had nothing to do with Justin's injuries. I do believe him in fact. But it's strange that Luke has just said exactly what Justin told me was the reason he beat him up.

Luke storms past me and heads for the door. He throws it open.

"Luke, wait …" I say, standing up, but he ignores me and leaves the office, and slams the door behind him leaving me standing there looking at the space where he stood only seconds ago.

I pushed him too far; I know I did. I should have been a better girlfriend and made it more clear to him that I believed him. As much as I do believe that Justin is my friend and only my friend, and for that reason, I want to defend him, given the choice, I would take Luke's side over his, and I don't think I showed that at all during that conversation.

What also convinces me that Luke is telling the truth is the fact that Louisa insists Justin is a creep. She didn't like him when we were dating, and she didn't like it when I decided to remain friends with him. When she found out he was in Chicago, she even said she thinks he only moved here because I did, and he wants to get back with me. Maybe there is some truth to it. Is it too much of a coincidence that the two people I am closest to both think the same thing about Justin? Am I somehow blind to his real motives?

I decide to give Luke a couple of hours to cool down or whatever it is he needs to do, and then I will come back this afternoon and apologize to him and make him see I do believe him, and I will stop seeing Justin if that's what he wants. I won't lose him over this. I can't bear the thought of it. I just have to hope that Luke is willing to forgive me.

I get up and leave his office, swallowing back tears. Whatever happens, I am not about to burst into tears at my place of work. I draw the line at that.

I go down to the web development team's working space, and I sit down and open up my laptop and go back to making the tweaks in the coding I've been working on. I force myself to concentrate only on my work and not let myself get distracted by any of my thoughts of Luke, and for the most part, I manage it, only looking up from my screen to greet Karl and the rest of the team as they come into work.

I'm making decent progress on my task, and I'm glad it's something I have to really concentrate on and not have a chance to let my mind wander.

"Louisa," Karl says, and I look up from my screen.

"Yeah," I say.

Karl laughs.

"That's like the third time I've called your name," he says.

"Sorry," I say.

"Don't apologize for being engrossed in your work," he says with a smile which I return.

I must have been deeper into my work than even I realized for him to have called me three times, but then again, it's easy to tune out background noise and still hear your name, but of course Louisa isn't my name. If he had said Tia, I probably would have acknowledged him the first time.

"Luke wants to see you," Karl says.

"Ok," I say. "Thanks. I'll go along on my lunch break."

Has he seen sense or is he going to tell me it's over between us and my internship with it?

"He said it's important and to tell you to go now," Karl adds.

"Oh, umm, ok," I say, and I lock my laptop screen and get up and head up to Luke's office.

I guess he's dumping me after all then because if he wasn't surely, he could have waited until my break and not demanded to see me now. I reach Luke's office door after smiling in at Mel, and I realize I'm once more on the verge of tears. I look up and blink them away and take a deep breath and then I knock on the door.

"Come in," Luke shouts.

I open the door and go inside and shut it quickly. If I'm about to be yelled at and dumped and fired, I don't need Mel to hear every word of it. I don't know if she knows we're together even, but I don't want her to have a front row seat to us ending things. Luke hasn't spoken yet and I go and sit down because my legs feel unsteady, and I don't want to embarrass myself by falling down.

I reach his desk and sit down, and he still hasn't spoken, although he has watched me walk towards him. I decide if he's going to remain silent, I'll get in first and apologize and hopefully change his mind about dumping me.

"I'm sorry," I say. "I do believe you, Luke. Honestly, I do. I know I didn't make that clear enough earlier, I realized that as soon as you left, but I promise you I do believe you."

"I think you want to believe me. I think maybe you even half believe me. But that's not enough Louisa," Luke says.

"No, honestly, I swear I believe you and I will tell Justin we can no longer be friends," I say.

I get up and go around to his side of the desk. I lean against it and look into Luke's eyes.

"How can I make it up to you?" I say. "And show you I believe you."

He looks back at me for a moment and then the corner of his lip curls up in a sexy smirk and he nods down into his lap and then raises an eyebrow. I know exactly what he wants, and I smile.

"What, here?" I say.

"Sure, why not? If anyone comes in, you'll be hidden by the desk," he says.

I grin at him.

"OK, but good luck acting normally, because I won't be stopping," I tease him.

I push off from the desk and get to my knees and Luke scoots his chair back. I get into the alcove beneath his desk, and he scoots his chair back in. I reach up and open his pants and I pull his cock out through the slit in his boxer shorts.

It's already hard and I lean down and run my tongue over the tip of it, holding the base of it in one fist. Luke moans and pre- cum drizzles out of the tip of his cock and I open my lips and put the tip in between them. I suck on it, swallowing down his juices and then I bob my head forward and run my lips down his length, sucking all of the time I do it. I suck again on my way back up and I get into a rhythm of bobbing my head up and down while sucking Luke hard.

I can tell by the noises he's making above me that he is getting close to his climax, and I smile around his cock when I hear someone knock on his office door.

"Stop," he hisses, and I do, but I stay in place.

He shuffles, trying to get his pants fastened, but I'm still holding the base of his cock, and he gives up and just calls for the person to come in. The door opens and then closes, and I hear Mel's voice.

"I thought I saw Louisa come in here," she says.

"Yeah, she did, but she's gone to the bathroom," Luke says.

I let him get halfway through his sentence and then I run my tongue up and down his length and swirl it around the tip of his cock once more. I hear the slight change in his voice and it's all I can do not to giggle as I suck him back into my mouth. I start sucking on him again, my head bobbing and my fist working in time with my mouth so that no part of his cock goes untouched.

"When she comes back, will you ask her to pop in to see me on her way out please," Mel says.

"Yes," Luke says. He bangs his fist on the table, and I picture Mel jumping. "Yes, I will."

"Umm are you ok?" Mel says. "You look a bit flushed and you're acting weird."

I hear her start to move closer.

"I'm fine," Luke almost shouts. I don't give him any

reprieve; the whole time he is talking to Mel I'm working his cock in my mouth. "Is that your phone ringing?"

"No, I don't think so," Mel says after a pause.

"Well, you best go and check," Luke says. "And I will send Louisa along when she comes back."

I hear the office door open and then close again and I still keep sucking Luke who moans loudly and comes in my mouth. I swallow down his seed and keep sucking, wanting to drink down every drop of his semen. I suck and swallow and suck and swallow until his cock softens and then I release him from my mouth.

Luke scoots his chair back, and I crawl out of the gap and stand up and then I perch on the desk beside him when he scoots back in. He looks at me with a grin and shakes his head.

"I can't believe you did that," he says.

"You seemed to be having such an enjoyable time. It seemed a shame to stop," I say.

He shakes his head again but he's laughing,

"I'm going to go out on a limb here and say Mel is probably suspicious about something happening between us at this point," he says.

"Or she just thinks you're absolutely mental," I add.

"Or that," Luke agrees.

"So, I'm forgiven then I take it?" I say.

"Of course," Luke says.

I stand up.

"I'd better get back to work then," I say.

"Wait, I haven't actually showed you what I called you here to show you," Luke says.

"Oh. I thought you called me here to dump me," I say.

"To dump you? What? Why would you think that?" Luke says and he looks genuinely puzzled.

"I didn't think I'd made it clear enough that I did believe

you," I say. "And I figured you didn't want to be with someone who doubted your word."

Luke thinks for moment and then he looks up at me.

"Admittedly, I did think you only half believed me, but I didn't want to dump you. I could understand from your point of view why you were struggling because Justin is your friend," Luke says. "I went to get proof to show you. I'm still going to show you it, but I'm glad that we had this conversation first, because now I know for sure you believed me fully before I show you this."

"I don't need to see it," I say. "Really."

"I know you don't need to see proof to believe me now, but aren't you curious about what really happened to Justin?" Luke says and I nod. I definitely am. He shows me a thumb drive. "This is CCTV from outside of the pub we went to. I went to talk to the owner. Don't tell anyone you've seen this because really, he's not supposed to give it out to anyone other than an officer of the law, but it's funny what promises of secrecy and a nice little cash incentive can make people do."

He puts the thumb drive into the side of his computer and clicks to play the file. He fiddles around until he finds out how to skip it forward, and he does this a few times.

"We're due to come out at any moment," he says.

I expect the images to be grainy, but they aren't at all. The damned thing is practically in HD. The door to the pub opens and I tense up, but it's a stranger. Seconds later, it opens again, and this time, Luke steps out. He looks both ways and then turns and starts to walk.

He reaches out and pauses the footage.

"I was going to call a cab, but I heard Justin coming behind me. He had already told me he was into you and all of that shit, that's why I walked away, and I didn't want to discuss it further and I figured I would walk at least so far home and flag down a cab and he would walk the other way and avoid any further confrontation," Luke explains and then he hits play again and the images start moving once more.

Luke walks a few more steps and then the pub door opens again and Justin steps out. He looks a bit unsteady on his feet but there's no bruising on his face. I wonder if he managed to fall and hurt himself, but that would be some epic fall to do that much damage to his face. I keep watching.

Justin stalks along behind Luke and then Luke turns around. There's no audio, but I see his mouth moving and he's pointing. Justin says something back and then he goes for Luke. Luke pushes him away before he can do any damage and then Luke turns around and walks away, leaving Justin leaning against the wall of the pub. Luke pauses the footage again.

"That's the last I saw of him. I walked the next block or two and flagged down a cab and went home," Luke says.

I look at the time on the display.

"That's only about half an hour before Justin arrived at my place. Say fifteen minutes for the cab ride. What the hell happened in the next fifteen minutes?" I say.

"Maybe he went back inside and got himself into trouble," Luke says.

"Let's see," I say.

Luke hits play again and for a moment, Justin just stands there and then he pushes himself up from the wall he's been leaning against. He stands in place swaying and then he says something which we can't hear. I gasp as I see what comes next. Justin punches himself in the face.

Luke and I look at each other in shock and then we both look back at the screen. Justin spends the next few minutes punching himself hard in the face, slamming his face off the side of the building, and just generally beating the hell out of himself. Finally, he stops the onslaught and gets his cell phone out which is, I assume, when he calls the cab to bring him to my place.

Luke reaches out and stops the footage.

"Well fuck. I didn't expect that," he says.

"Me neither," I say. "God he's a real fucking psycho, isn't he?"

Luke nods his head.

"It's not normal to go to those lengths to get someone to break up with their partner so he can muscle his way in," he says. "I know he's your friend and I would never say you can't be friends with someone, but please Louisa, promise me you won't see him alone."

"There's no way I want to be friends with him after this," I say. "It's … far too much."

"That's a nice way of wording it," Luke says, and we both laugh, and I feel a bit better, although I still feel a pit of dread in my stomach. Justin isn't normal. Luke warned me about him and Louisa warned me about him, and I chose to ignore both of them, only to see for myself what a giant creep Justin is. I'm glad I've seen it for myself now though so I can make sure to cut off all ties with him. "Are you ok?"

"Yeah," I say. "I'm just a bit freaked out that I was ever friends with this guy. I'm glad now that Emily left him for her sake. Oh wait, they might get back together, I should warn her."

"They aren't getting back together. Justin refused to apologize to her," Luke says. "He told me before he turned weird."

"That's something at least," I say. "I have to get back now; Karl will think I got lost. What should I tell him you wanted?"

"A blow job," Luke says.

"Ha ha very funny," I say.

"I thought so," Luke grins. "Just say we were discussing your progress as an intern and that I'm very happy with your work and that you're happy on the team. Assuming you are happy there?"

"I am," I confirm.

"Don't forget to pop in and see what Mel wants on the way out," Luke says, and I feel myself blushing just at the thought of it.

"I hope she hasn't been watching for me coming back from the bathroom," I say.

"Don't worry," Luke says. "Even if she has put the pieces together, she's discreet."

# CHAPTER
## Thirty-Two

**TIA**

It's my lunch break and I've eaten my tuna salad bowl and a chocolate muffin. I pick up my cell phone and search through my contacts for Justin's name. I find him and touch the screen and choose text message. I was going to call him and ask for an explanation for what happened, but I have decided that there isn't anything he can say that I will accept as a plausible reason for what he did. For that reason, I have also decided that he doesn't deserve a phone call. He can have a text message and he's only getting that because I want him to know that I know what he's done and that I choose Luke over him and would do the same thing a thousand times over.

I stare at the blank screen of my cell phone for a few seconds while I gather my thoughts and then I start to type.

"I know Luke didn't do that to your face. I know what you did, and I can't be friends with someone who could do something like that and then lie about it. I wish you well, but please don't contact me again," my text message says.

I reread it and I hit send. I was careful not to say I'm sorry we can't be friends anymore or anything along those lines because while it might have softened the blow a bit, if Justin thinks there's even a small part of me that's sorry to see him go, I don't think he will leave me alone. I do think the bit where I wish him well might soften the blow a bit and stop him from replying and being argumentative though.

It doesn't stop him from replying. Within seconds of me hitting send, my cell phone beeps, alerting me to a new text message. I already know who it will be from, and I reluctantly pick up my cell phone. I half and half want to just ignore it, but I know I won't be able to put this behind me until I have read his reply. I open the message.

"Please don't do this Tee. I know I was a fool, and I regret what I did. I know it's no excuse, but I was drunk and drunk me thought it was a good idea. Sober me would never have done such a thing. I only did it because I love you though. Forgive me. Be mine once more and I will spend forever making this up to you I swear x," the message says.

It's actually a lot less aggressive than what I was expecting, but it has no more effect on me than if he had told me to fuck off. There was a time if he had told me he loved me, I would've had some sympathy for him at least, but not now. Not after what he's done. I can't feel anything for him but a deep dislike.

I start to reply to the text message, but I decide against it. Every reply Justin gets, regardless of what I say, will only spur him on. If he thinks I'm still bothering to reply to him, he will think there's a part of me that still cares about him, a part he can manipulate into coming around to his side of things. There isn't and there's nothing he can say to make me feel sorry for him now, but I really don't have the energy to waste on arguing with him. I lock my cell phone screen and put it back away.

By the time I've cleaned up after myself in the break room, there's another two messages beeped in. By the time I've used the ladies' room and headed back to my workstation, another one. By the time Karl tells me to either answer my cell phone or put it on silent, another four messages have come in.

I apologize to Karl and pull my cell phone out. I switch it to silent and take a quick look at the messages. All of them are from Justin as I suspected and all of them are variations of him telling me he's sorry, he loves me, and he doesn't want to lose me from his life. He even offers to apologize to Luke. I put my cell phone back away without replying. If he keeps going, I will just block his number.

I check my cell phone again an hour or so later and I see that having it on silent has lulled me into a false sense of security. There are over thirty messages now. I don't have time to read all of those right now and I don't know if I want to. I open the last one and I instantly wish I hadn't. Justin has gone from trying to get me to come around to threatening me.

"Watch your back Tee because this isn't over. I will do whatever it takes to get you back and if that means making your world burn to do it, trust me, I have a match," the message says.

I block Justin's number and put my cell phone away. I start to feel better pretty much as soon as I start working again. Justin is just blowing off steam. He can't make my world burn because the only two people in my world who know him wouldn't trust him as far as they can throw him.

Now, he's blocked, and I won't have to see any more of his bullshit messages. I can just concentrate on work and tonight, I'm going to Luke's place for dinner. When I'm not concentrating on the lines and lines of code in front of me, I will focus on that.

# CHAPTER
## Thirty-Three

**LUKE**

I'm going about my afternoon when there's a knock on my office door and when I shout come in, Mel comes in.

"Sorry to bother you," she says. "But there's someone here to see you. He doesn't have an appointment, but he says he's a personal friend and it's important."

I can't think of which of my friends would drop into my place of work to tell me something, even something important, without at least calling me first.

"Did you get this person's name?" I say.

"Justin Martin," Mel says. "Should I send him away?"

My first instinct is to say yes, but for Justin to have made the effort to come here, I must admit he has my interest piqued. What does he possibly have to say to me at this point?

"No, I'll see him," I say.

"Ok," Mel says.

She ducks out of the door, leaving it ajar and I hear her

walking away. She returns a few minutes later and opens the door wider.

"Mr Martin to see you," she says, and she gestures with her hand and Justin steps into my office.

"Thanks Mel," I say, and she nods to me and closes the door. I turn my attention to Justin. His face is a mess and I almost wince when I think about how painful it must be, but then I remind myself he did this to himself and tried to frame me for it and any empathy I was feeling for him disappears. "I didn't expect to see you here."

"I would have called, but I didn't think you'd answer," he says.

"You're probably right," I concede. I nod at the chair opposite mine. "Why don't you take a seat and tell me why you're here."

Justin walks over and sits down. He clenches his hands together on my desk in front of himself. He smiles at me, an awkward smile that doesn't reach his eyes.

"I'm not sure where to start or even if I should be here," he says.

I shrug one shoulder. I don't particularly want him here and I don't want him to feel encouraged to keep dropping in, but I do want to know why he's here.

"Start at the beginning," I say.

"Her. She was the beginning. I fell in love with her the moment I saw her. I know that sounds crazy, but I did. I couldn't believe it when I asked her out and she said yes. I thought we were good together, but she had other ideas, and I see now that she manipulated me into loving her and then she dumped me like trash but kept me on her hook. She's toxic Luke. That's what I'm saying. I see it now. I wish I had seen it earlier, and I wish that someone she had destroyed before me had warned me. So here I am warning you," he says.

I feel myself starting to get angry. This pathetic little man has lost Louisa, and this is his last resort. To try to ruin things for us so she feels as empty as he does. Maybe he even thinks that she will go back to him eventually if I'm out of the picture.

"That's enough, Justin," I say.

"No, it's not, because you don't believe me," he says.

"Does it matter?" I reply. "You've done your bit by telling me. Your conscience is clear."

"She's lying to you, you know. About everything," he says.

I know I shouldn't bite, but I can't help it.

"I think there's only one liar in this and that's you," I say.

"She didn't tell you I'm her ex-boyfriend, did she? Not until I let it slip at the restaurant that night," he says.

"No," I say. "But not because of any reason except it's irrelevant. Do you think I have sat and told Louisa about every girl I ever dated?"

"Tia," he says. "Her name is Tia, not Louisa."

"No, that's your little pet name for her," I say.

"No, it isn't. That's the cover story I used when I slipped up and called her Tia in front of you. She …" he is still talking but I talk over him.

"That's enough," I say. "I think it's time for you to leave."

"Because you're starting to wonder, aren't you?" he says. "Come on. Do you really think that girl is a Sanchez? She is about as Latina as I am."

I want to tell him he's being ridiculous, but is he? I mean he's certainly not wrong about her not looking like a Sanchez.

"So what? This is just some girl off the street that heard Louisa had an internship here and decided to take over her life and her job? So where is the real Louisa in all of this?" I say.

"She's not just some random girl. Tia and the real Louisa

are best friends, and this is some scheme they cooked up between them. Honestly, I said Tia is manipulative and she is, but she isn't near as good as Louisa," Justin says.

I don't want to believe him, but little things are starting to add up. Like how she told me Sophia wouldn't acknowledge her in the board meeting. It wasn't because she didn't want to draw attention to them being sisters, it was because Sophia isn't her damned sister. She probably doesn't even know her. And all of the times someone has called her name, and she hasn't replied and then pretended she was miles away. Is that because Louisa isn't her real name, and she didn't realize they meant her. It even happened on her first day when I called on her in the meeting to stand up. And that time Enrique wanted to talk to her on the phone and she ran from the room rather than speaking to him. Did she really have to use the bathroom, or did she just not want the ruse to be up?

I hate to think badly of her, especially after Justin set me up and I felt the pain of having Louisa – Tia? – only half believe me, but it does all make sense. And why would Justin come up with such a ridiculous lie if it isn't true? If he wanted to say something to make me think Louisa is a bad person, surely, he could have chosen a less far out there lie.

"I can see that you're starting to believe me. Do you want more proof? I can call the real Louisa right now," Justin says.

"Just get out," I say. "Get out of my office. Get out of my building and never come back unless you want to leave in handcuffs."

Justin stands up and he has the sheer audacity to smile down at me.

"I'll leave," he says. "You were right earlier. My conscience is clear now. If you're cool with going along with someone who has done nothing but lie to you, that's on your head now."

He turns and walks away, and I quickly call through to Mel.

"Make sure that man leaves the building. Follow him. If he doesn't go straight out, don't approach him, just call me," I say.

"Is everything ok?" Mel asks.

"Just go," I say.

I wait a few minutes and the knock I'm expecting comes. I call to come in and Mel comes in, her face a mask of concern.

"Who was that guy? Are you alright? You look … I don't know. Shocked!" Mel says. "He left by the way."

"Sit down," I say.

Mel sits down and I find myself telling her everything that's happened with Louisa and me and where Justin fits into it all, and then his accusation about her not being who she says she is.

"What do you think?" I ask.

"I don't know what to think," Mel says. "There have been occasions where Louisa hasn't responded to her name the first time to me too, and that time Enrique called and she ran from you, she put him through without going through me and I went to remind her not to do that, but then she said the caller was Enrique. I was surprised because I never would have suspected the caller was her father the way she was so formal. She gave me the line about separating family and business, but it struck me as odd. But her pretending to be someone else all seems a bit too Twilight Zone for me."

"What do you think I should do? Hire someone to look into her background?" I say.

Mel thinks for a moment.

"How serious are you about her?" she asks.

"I'm in love with her," I say.

"So will this make any difference either way?" Mel asks.

I nod.

"Yes. I can't see myself being with someone who has lived a lie the whole time we've known each other," I say.

"But assuming Justin is lying, you want to stay with her?" Mel says and I nod.

"Yes, of course," I say.

"Then don't hire anyone. Ask her yourself. You'll know by her reaction whether she is lying or not. And if she's not, you two can have a laugh about it and you won't lose her. If you hire someone and she finds out, you're done," Mel says.

"Thanks Mel," I say. "That's sound advice."

"I have my uses," Mel says with a grin. "Do you want me to call down and have her come up and talk to you?"

"Yes please," I say.

I wait until Mel has left the room and closed the door behind her and then I start pacing back and forth in my office while I wait. I have a really bad feeling about this, but I have to know for sure if it's true or not, and I do think Mel was right about the problem with hiring someone to find the answers for me. Also, that takes time, and Louisa would know straight away that something was off with me.

I stop pacing and go and sit back down when there's a knock on my office door. I want to look like I'm calm and in control of this situation, even though I feel like I'm the complete opposite of both of those things.

"Come in," I say, and Louisa comes in and smiles at me.

"Sit down," I say, and her smile turns into a frown I presume because of the cold tone of voice I used on her.

She sits down.

"What's up?" she says.

"I've just had Justin in here telling me how you're toxic and he wished someone would have warned him to stay away from you right from the start," I say.

"The same Justin who beat the shit out of himself and blamed you for it," Louisa points out.

I nod.

"Yes. And at that point, I told him to get out of my office, but then he said something else. Something so crazy I should have just laughed him out of the building. Except I have to admit that parts of it made sense … Tia," I say.

I wait for her to ask who the hell Tia is, or why I'm using Justin's pet name for her, but she doesn't. Instead, she just stares at me for a second and then her face crumples and she covers it with her hands as tears spring from her eyes. I hate the fact that she's crying, and I really hate the fact that I'm the one who made her cry, but I guess it's confirmation of what Justin told me being true.

I give her a minute to get herself under control and when she sniffles and uncovers her face, I hand her a tissue. She takes it and wipes her eyes and then blows her nose. She looks more like herself again except for her red nose and blotchy cheeks.

"Start talking," I say.

"Louisa is my best friend. Her father wanted her to do this internship. She didn't want to do it. I needed a job and so we came up with the idea of me pretending to be her," Louisa, sorry Tia, says. "It sounds so silly now, but at the time, it made perfect sense. I'm so sorry for lying to you about who I was, but I had never even met you when we concocted the plan. I never would have dreamed we'd end up dating and I did try so hard to stay away from you that way. I hoped I could finish my internship, then come clean with you and see where things went from there."

"So, our whole time together, you've been someone else," I say, trying and failing to get my head around that.

"No," Tia says, shaking her head. "No, it's not like that. I have been using someone else's name, but that's it. The rest of it is the real me. I've never actually pretended to be Louisa.

You know that yourself because Enrique warned you what Louisa would be like, and I am nothing like that."

"I don't even know what to say," I admit.

"Say you'll forgive me," Tia says. "Even if you can't do it right now. Say you'll forgive me in time, and that we can get past this."

"As much as I would like to say that I can't, because it's not true," I say. "I just … I can't even look at you," I say and that's the truth. The thought of her not being in my life hurts like fuck, but the idea of staying with her and knowing she lied to me all of this time is too much. I can't do it.

"Luke, please …" Tia says, and tears are running down her face again, but I can't let them sway me. I shake my head.

"I'm sorry Tia. Really, I am, but we're done here. Don't make it any harder than it needs to be," he says. "And don't bother coming back to work tomorrow either. I will see that you get your last paycheck."

She opens her mouth to argue with me I assume, but instead, all that comes out is a sob. She slaps her hand over her mouth and gets up and practically runs to my door. She opens it.

"I really am sorry," she says and then she leaves and closes the door behind her, and I feel as though my whole life has fallen apart with the closing of the door.

The imagery of her closing the door to me as I closed my heart to her isn't lost on me and it does nothing to make me feel better. I have to keep myself under control because I have a feeling Mel will be along in a minute to see if I'm ok, and then once I've dealt with her, I'm going to leave early and maybe go for a run or go to the gym or something to get rid of all of this pent-up anger and upset.

∽

Mel has been in, and I gave an Oscar worthy performance of convincing her that I am totally ok. She finally accepted it and left my office. My leaving early is probably going to set her off again, but I'd rather that than sit here stewing. I stand up and go to grab my jacket when my desk phone rings. I almost ignore it, but I just can't do it – it must be something important for Mel to have connected the call, especially now - and I find myself picking up the receiver.

"Hello," I say.

"Don't you hello me you fucking clown," my caller says.

I'm taken aback for a moment. I mean how else would I answer their call but with a hello? And why the rudeness? It hits me that the caller is Enrique, and I get a sinking feeling in my stomach. I guess I'm not the only person Justin has dropped a Tia shaped bomb on today.

"Enrique," I say, and I have no idea where I'm going after that. I don't want to say too much in case something else has happened that I don't know about, and I drop this on him myself. I'm actually grateful when he interrupts me, although I'm not happy about what he has to say.

"I ask for one simple favor, and this is the best you can do. You're a fool and I will be calling an emergency board meeting as soon as I'm back in the country and you will be fired, I guarantee it," Enrique says.

"But ..." I start, but the dial tone sounds in my ear. Enrique has ended the call. I sigh and replace the receiver.

I would love to know how the fuck Enrique has decided this is my fault, but I guess he needs someone to blame and it's not going to be his precious princess, and it wouldn't be a good look for him to go after Tia either. So, I get the shit. Me, who built this company from the ground up, going to be removed from my position at the helm of it. We'll fucking see about that.

I grab my jacket and put it on and grab my things and get

out of my office before anything else can stop me. I pop my head around Mel's door and tell her to hold my calls and that I'll see her tomorrow. I don't give her a chance to start asking if I'm ok again. I say goodbye to Rachel on the way past and she replies and then I'm in the elevator and then I'm down to the lobby. I cross it and get in my car, and I feel safe here that I won't have to talk to anyone else. I slam my hands on my steering wheel.

"Fuck," I shout as I do it. I do it again. "Fuck."

I pull my cell phone out and send a text to Tia.

"Congratulations. It's not just you getting fired because of this mess you caused. You're taking me down with you," I write.

I don't even know why I sent it. It's not like she wanted to get me fired. I guess I'm just being a bit petty. I feel bad because of something she did so I want to make her feel bad too. Her reply comes in fast.

"I'll fix this. I promise," it says.

I don't bother to reply.

# CHAPTER
## Thirty-Four

**TIA**

I texted Louisa earlier and asked if I could come to her place and talk to her, but she said she was out and that she would come to mine once she was done. It's just after six o'clock and she's here now. I kind of hoped to catch her within the working day so I could ask for her help in getting her father to not fire Luke. Whatever consequences there are for Louisa and me are deserved because we did this. Luke did nothing wrong.

I press the unlock button on the intercom and open my front door and wait for Louisa to come up. I can hear her heels clicking on the stairs and then she's there and I feel tears prickle in the corners of my eyes at the sight of her.

"The shit has really hit the fan Lou," I say.

"Yeah, tell me about it," she says.

She comes towards me, and I think she's going to hug me, but instead, she just walks past me and goes into my living room. I close my front door and start to follow her, but then I think of a better idea, and I pop to the kitchen and grab a bottle of left over Chablis from my book club meeting and two glasses and then I go to the living room. Louisa and I sit in silence while I pour the drinks and then I finally force myself to look at her.

"How did you find out?" I say.

"My father called me. I missed his call, but he left a voice mail giving me the basic gist of it. I haven't called him back yet. I figured it would make sense to get the full story first. So, what happened?" Louisa asks.

"Justin fucking happened. You were right about him. He wanted to get back with me, and when I refused, he decided to implode my whole life," I say.

"Wait, I don't get it. How did Justin know?" Louisa says. My face must say it all. "Oh, I see."

"I'm sorry. It just kind of slipped out," I say.

Louisa shrugs.

"It's ok. You thought you could trust him. But I still don't get how he thought getting you fired would make you want to get back with him," Louisa says.

Here comes the tough part. I take a big gulp of wine.

"Well, you see, the thing is, I don't think that was his main aim. I've been seeing Luke, and Justin wanted to break us up. He tried …" I'm saying when Louisa cuts in, her face a mask of anger.

"Wait. You're dating Luke? While he thinks you're me?" she snaps.

I nod.

"I wanted to tell you, but I didn't know how you would react," I say.

"Do you know Neil and I nearly broke up because of you?" Louisa says. She's getting really angry now. "He half knows Luke. They move in similar circles. And he heard a rumor that Luke and I were dating. He thought I was cheating on him. In the end, the only way I could prove my innocence was to tell him the truth – that Luke doesn't even know who I am and if anyone asked him, he would point to you."

"I'm so sorry," I say. "God I've really messed everything up."

I try to stop myself from crying, but I can't. Sobs wrack my body, and I just want to go to bed and curl up in a ball and stay there.

"No, come on Tee, don't cry," Louisa says. "I'm sorry. I know this was my idea not yours so if anything, all of this is my fault."

"I'm the one who told Justin," I say.

"And I'm the one who talked you into doing it," Louisa says. She smiles at me. "How about we agree that we both fucked up?"

I smile back and nod.

"Are you and Neil ok now?" I ask.

"No," Louisa says. "But it's not because of this. We just kind of fizzled out."

"I'm sorry," I say.

"I'm not," Louisa says. "Let's not waste any more time talking about him. That's another mess that's been cleaned up, just like this one."

"What am I going to do about Luke though," I say.

"I can save his job easily enough. Let me talk to my father real quick, and as for you two being together, I guess you just have to hope he likes you more than he hates what you've done," Louisa says.

It's all I can do really, but I kind of hoped Louisa would have some miracle solution for me. I top up our glasses and sit back and sip my wine while Louisa gets her cell phone out and calls her father.

"Hi Daddy," she says, putting the call on speaker phone. "How's Europe?"

"Never mind bloody Europe girl. I know about the stunt you pulled. And I say you because I don't blame Tia for a second. I know this was all you," he says.

I feel a bit better for that one. At least Enrique isn't mad at me too.

"I can explain," Louisa says. "I know you think I'm work shy or whatever, but that just isn't true."

"And you thought having someone pretend to be you and doing the job I got for you would prove this, did you?" he snaps, not sounding convinced. I have to say he makes a good point, but Louisa isn't done yet.

"That's it, though. The job you got for me. I would have always felt like I was being judged as your daughter rather than as myself. So, I found my own internship and I didn't tell you because I was afraid that I would fail, so I let you think I was doing the one you got me, and I haven't failed. I have actually got an offer from them too and I'm trying to choose between them. And I knew Tia needed an internship as much as I did so I offered her the one you got me," she says.

My mouth drops open. God she's good.

"But why didn't you just tell me Tia was taking the internship? Do you think I would have stood in her way?" Enrique says.

"No, but you would have demanded to know why I wasn't taking it," she says. "I'm really sorry I lied, but I hope you understand why I did it."

Enrique sighs.

"I understand," he says, and he actually sounds pleased when he goes on. "So, you have two offers now?"

"Yes," Louisa says. "I'm kind of hoping you can give me some advice on which one to take when you come home."

"My clever girl. Of course I will," he says.

"One other thing," Louisa says. "Please don't fire Luke.

He had no idea about any of this. I mean what would you have said on Tia's first day if he had called you and basically said this girl is too white to be your daughter and you had adopted her or something?"

"Ok, ok, point taken," Enrique says. "I won't fire Luke. And seeing as Tia is almost my adopted daughter at this point anyway, I don't want any of the money back."

"What money?" Louisa says.

"The wages. The internship was unpaid, but I knew you would never agree to do that, so I paid the wages," he says.

I gasp and put my hand over my mouth.

"Oh my God, I swear I will pay the money back Mr Sanchez," I say.

"Oh, you're here Tia," he says. "You will do no such thing, and let's drop the Mr Sanchez thing ok? Like I said, you're practically family girl."

"O … OK," I stutter. "Thank you so much."

"No more scheming you two, ok?" he says.

We both laugh and promise him no more schemes and then he and Louisa say their goodbyes and she ends the call.

"I feel awful now," I say.

"About the money?" Louisa asks and I nod. "Look I'm not trying to knock what my dad has done because I think it's very sweet of him, but it's pocket change to him Tee. Don't worry about it."

"It's not that. I mean he's giving me that money and we're still lying to him," I say.

"Oh God, what haven't you told me?" Louisa says.

"Nothing," I say. "I meant your internship and second job offer."

"Oh, that's true," Louisa says. "It's why I'm never around when you call me through the working day."

"Oh wow. You dark horse," I laugh. "Congratulations."

I clink my glass off hers and we drink.

"I'll text Luke and tell him his job is safe," I say. "At least that bit is corrected. Now I just have to get him to forgive me and find a new job and everything is good."

"To everything being good again," Louisa says, raising her glass again. We clink again, but this time, it doesn't really feel like a celebration to me.

# CHAPTER
## Thirty-Five

**LUKE**

M y cell phone pings, and I take it out of my pocket. It's a text message from Tia which I almost ignore, but I decide to read it. I also decide it's time to change her name from Louisa in my contacts list. I almost change it to liar, but I can't bring myself to do it, and I just put Tia and then I go and read her text.

"Louisa and I have spoken to Enrique. He has calmed down and sees this isn't your fault and he's not going to try and get you fired. Also, I had no idea he was personally paying my wages, but he has said he doesn't want the money back," her text message says.

I ponder this for a moment. I was going to send Enrique the money myself, but I had no intention of taking it from Tia. She earned every cent of that money, and it should be hers. This gets me to thinking. Personally, I can never trust her again because she lied to my face about her identity. But professionally, she has been such an asset to the team, and I know Karl wants her as a permanent fixture.

The main reason I was holding back from making her a job offer was because we were dating, but now we're not and if I separate the personal from the professional, I can see that I should do what I can to keep Tia working with the company.

I think for a minute and then I start to write a text back to Tia.

"OK, thanks for the head's up. I feel like I overreacted slightly throwing you out of the building earlier. Would you be willing to come in tomorrow morning for a meeting with me?"

I hit send before I change my mind and the response comes quickly.

"Of course. What time?"

I text back and tell her nine thirty am and when she texts back thanking me, I don't reply any more. I wouldn't say anything further to any other employee at the end of such a conversation and I have to start thinking of Tia as just another employee.

A knock comes on my office door at fourteen minutes past nine am and I don't know how I feel about it. I have butterflies in my stomach at the thought of seeing Tia again after thinking yesterday I would never see her again, but I have to remain firm and not let her beauty get to me. I take a deep breath and call out for her to come in.

She opens the door, comes in and closes it behind her. She stands in the center of the floor for a moment, and she looks so lost that I want to go to her and hold her in my arms and tell her I'll be her anchor, that she will never be lost again. But I can't. I won't.

She's wearing a royal blue shift dress and heels. Simple, professional, and on her, absolutely gorgeous. It brings out the blue of her eyes and her white-blonde hair sits on her shoulders, looking even shinier than ever against the darker back drop. Am I really going to just let this girl leave my life? I don't want to, but I have to. How can I be with someone that I don't trust to tell me the truth? How can I be with someone who I doubt every time she speaks? It's simple. I can't. It wouldn't be fair to either of us.

"Sit down," I say, and she does, sitting on her hands like a child. "Would you like a drink?"

"I could use a triple gin right about now," she says, and she smiles and despite myself I smile with her. "But no thank you."

"Then let's get down to why I asked you to come here today," I say. "Throughout your time here, you have impressed both me and Karl with your work ethic and your skills. I would be crazy to have you walk away from the company without at least trying to get you to stay."

"You want me to complete the internship?" she says. "I would love that, because I feel like I've let Karl down by not finishing the task he gave me."

"I don't want you to complete the internship. I've seen enough," I say. "I'm offering you a full time position on the web development team. If you accept, you can hash the details out with HR."

"Have you ever offered an intern a position half way through their time before?" she asks.

The question throws me for a second, but I answer it. I shake my head.

"No," I say.

"Then I must decline the offer. I don't want any special treatment," she says.

I shake my head.

"This isn't special treatment because of what you and I had," I say. "I'm making this offer because you're an asset to the company. It's not just me saying so, it's Karl too. He was begging me to make you an offer within a few days of you working with him."

"Really?" Tia says.

"Really," I confirm. "The only thing that stopped me was because we were dating, and I felt like it might be weird. I planned on talking to you after your internship was up about it, but here we are. And just to further put your mind at ease, if I was basing this off of our personal relationship, I wouldn't let you within a mile of the company, but basing it purely off your work, the job is yours if you want it."

# CHAPTER
## Thirty-Six

**TIA**

The job offer from Luke is amazing, but his final words really burst the bubble of excitement inside of me. Not so much the part about him not trusting me based on our personal relationship – I completely get why he would feel that way right now – but the part about how he hadn't offered me a job because we were dating, which implies he doesn't date staff, and now he is offering me the job, which makes me think he is pretty much saying there is no hope for us.

For that reason, I want to turn the job down. To tell him that I want that door to be kept open for us, that I will do anything to make him forgive me, but the truth is, I can't afford to do that unless I want to be homeless. Plus, it would feel like a kick in the teeth to Enrique too who has basically paid my wages for the time I've been here to just walk away now.

"Then I accept the offer. Thank you," I say.

"After this conversation, there can be no mention of us

dating. We will have the same relationship as any two people who work together. But first, I have to ask you one thing," Luke says. He looks at me and I nod for him to go on. "I get why you and Louisa did what you did in some ways. And I can understand that you felt no loyalty towards me at that time. But once we started dating, why didn't you tell me the truth then? Did you not trust me?"

"I trust you with my life," I say, purposely using the present tense to let Luke know he might have given up on us, but my feelings for him are still very much there. "I wanted to tell you so badly, but I had to push the idea away, because I knew if I did tell you, even if you took it well, I couldn't possibly stay working here as Louisa once I told you because that would implicate you in the lie."

"And I'm not Louisa. I'm not a trust fund kid. I don't know my father and my mom died while I was at college, so I have no one to fall back on. If I left this job, I would have essentially been making myself homeless," I say.

"Ok, I guess I understand your fear. And I want to be able to move past it, but I can't. Never the less, I'm sorry about your mom and about your situation. I had no idea," he says.

I smile sadly at him.

"I could never tell you. But I guess none of that matters now," I say.

"No, I guess not," Luke agrees.

For a moment, he looks sad, and I just want to hold him, but I know he won't welcome my touch and so I stay where I am, and the moment passes, and Luke is all business again.

"Go and get on with your work. Tell Karl you're late because I was making you a job offer. Make his day. I'll call down to HR and get the ball rolling and they'll be in touch when they have a contract put together," he says. "And it will be in your true name, so I suggest you start telling people who you really are. Tia...?"

"Lake," I say.

He jots it down and then he just looks at me without saying anything else and I stand up, aware that I'm being dismissed.

"Thank you," I say again and then I stop talking, because there is so much I want to say and none of it is appropriate and I'm scared if I say so much as another word, it will all just spill out of me. I don't want to make Luke regret giving me this chance and so I scurry from his office without a backwards glance.

# CHAPTER
## Thirty~Seven

**LUKE**

It's been almost two weeks since everything fell apart with Tia and me. I have purposely avoided her where I can at work, getting only progress reports from Karl who continues to be pleased with her work. We have had another one today and I have told him he doesn't have to keep coming to me now, that Tia is a member of staff, and he will be responsible for her just like the rest of his team.

I miss her so much, and the thing is, the more time passes, the more I think that I could get past her lying about her identity, because when I think about it, the only lies she told me were her name and that Enrique and Sophia were her family but from what I've gathered after the event, Tia is as good as a part of their family, so it literally is just her name she lied about.

No one but me seems to have a problem with it. It's kind of a running joke between Tia and the rest of the staff and even Enrique seems to be in on the joke. He called yesterday and was laughing as he asked how his surrogate daughter was settling into her new role. I know none of these people have such an intimate relationship with Tia as I had, but even so, I'm really starting to think that I overreacted.

Of course, I overreacted. I see it clearly now. I want Tia back, and I don't care about the stupid lie she told when she didn't even know me. I know everything else about her was genuinely her, and I really feel like this woman is my soul mate. I'm not going to lose the love of my life over something so stupid as my own stubbornness.

The trouble is, I have made a ton of effort to avoid her, and she must have noticed that. And when our speaking to each other has been unavoidable, I haven't exactly been nice to her. I haven't been awful either, I've been cold and indifferent, and I think that can be worse than being horrible. Being horrible would have showed her I still felt something for her – hence the reason I didn't do it – but cold indifference must have made her think I've moved on.

God, I hope she hasn't moved on and found someone else. In some ways, I think it would serve me right if she had, but I'm not going to let myself even consider it. I know if I want her to take me back, I'm going to have to do something epic to make her be able to get past the way I have treated her since we broke up.

I wonder if Mel has any ideas of what I could do. I'm sure she will have. I go to stand up, but then a better idea comes to me, and I text Enrique asking him for Louisa's number saying I want her advice on something. He sends it to me, and I write out a text to Louisa.

"This is Luke Jackson. I've been an idiot, and I need your help. I'm in love with Tia, and I want her back, but I'm afraid I may have waited too long. Do you have any idea what I can say or do to win her back?"

I reread the message and send it, crossing my fingers that I get a reply, and that Louisa agrees to help me. I'm starting to think she's just going to ignore me when a text comes in and I see it's from her. I read it quickly.

"It took you long enough to work that out! Luckily for you, Tia is still very much into you, and you have me to help make this reunion special for her. Meet me at the mall at six. We need a few things to make this work. Oh, and if you ever hurt my best friend again, I will cut your balls off," the message says.

I can feel my smile growing wider the more I read. Tia still likes me and Louisa, her best friend, thinks I have a chance and she's willing to help me. Even when she threatens to cut my balls off, I'm happy. Tia deserves a best friend who will do that for her, and I will never ever hurt that girl again, so my balls are safe.

"I'll be there," I write and send it back.

# CHAPTER
## Thirty-Eight

**TIA**

I've just got into my car to head home from work. I'm looking forward to a weekend of chilling out in my pajamas, watching movies, eating junk food and wishing I was with Luke. I know it's kind of pathetic at this point, but I just can't let go of him. It probably doesn't help that I work at his company, but we really don't see that much of each other there and when we do, we speak to each other like we're strangers and God that hurts me. I would rather Luke shout and scream at me and tell me how much I hurt him than him just be cold to me. But I brought this on myself, and I understand that I don't get to tell him how to handle it. I just wish I could make him be mine again, but it's probably too late to even try now. Even if he somehow decided he could forgive me, he probably has a new girlfriend by now.

I can't stand the thought of that, but it's still likely a reality. I turn the radio on and blast the music to try and drown out my thoughts and I put my car in drive and head home. I stop off at a fried chicken place and get a bargain bucket and then I drive straight home.

I go inside and go to my apartment. I change into my pajamas, put some chicken and some fries on a plate, and then I go and choose a movie to watch while I eat. I want to watch something scary or an action style movie, but I find myself drawn to the romantic comedies, another rather annoying side effect of my breakup. I'm turning into such a cliché. I might as well just give in, buy a tub of ice cream, and eat the whole thing while crying.

I've just about finished my food when my cell phone pings. It's a text from Louisa. I open it and read it.

"Hey you. No more moping. I've left you to wallow in self-pity for as long as I can. There's a party on my building's rooftop. Nothing too wild, just some friends having drinks and relaxing and you're coming. Meet me up there at eight or I'm coming to your place to drag you here," the text says.

It's typical Louisa and my instinct is to reply telling her I don't want to come to a party, I don't feel ready for a party, I know she won't accept no for an answer when she gets to this stage, and she will go through on her promise and come and get me and drag me there if I don't show up. In the long run, it will be easier and much less embarrassing to just go. I can show my face, have a drink or two, and then make my excuses and leave. Or maybe I can actually just stay and have fun. That's probably pushing it a bit. Another text message pings in.

"Dress to impress. Love you."

"I'll be there. Love you too," I send back.

Considering it's only supposed to be a few friends chilling with a drink, I fail to see why I need to dress up. Oh yes, because Louisa is lying. Her building's rooftop parties are always packed with people.

I poke my last French fry into my mouth and chew it slowly and then I check the time. It's almost seven o'clock and so I get up and go and shower. I dry my hair and put my makeup on and then I debate what to wear. I choose a short black dress with a puff ball bottom and shiny black heels. I add silver earrings, necklace and bracelet to the look, and spritz myself with perfume and I'm good to go.

I get a silver purse from my closet and then I go to the living room and transfer my wallet to the purse. I call a cab and then slip my cell phone into the purse. I leave the apartment and add my keys to my purse, and I'm good to go. I go downstairs to the lobby to wait for the cab. I don't have long to wait.

We pull up outside of Louisa's building and I pay the driver and get out. Louisa's building is a lot better than mine, and it even has a door attendant. He knows me now and he smiles a greeting and releases the door lock for me.

"Good evening, Tia," he says. "You look nice tonight."

"Thanks Stan, good to see you," I say.

I go to the elevator and get in and I hit the button for the roof. The elevator goes up and up and up, eventually pinging open on the rooftop. The air is chillier up here and I shiver slightly but I will soon warm up when I get a drink or two into me. It's that thought that makes me realize I've stepped out of the elevator onto an empty rooftop. There's no music, no bar, no people. I step away from the tower where the elevator shaft resides and look around.

Behind me, the rooftop is covered in pretty white fairy lights. I wonder if Louisa is hosting this party, and she has asked me to come early to help her set up. I start to walk toward the fairy lights and soft music starts to play.

From seemingly nowhere, but obviously from the shadowy edge of the roof, a figure emerges. For a second, I think it's Louisa, but it's not, it's Luke. He's dressed in a suit and a white shirt and it's not like his work suits. It's a proper black tie style suit. He comes towards me, and I stop, not knowing what's going on or what I'm meant to be doing.

He closes the gap between us some and when he's a few feet away from me, he gets down on one knee. I gasp and put my hand over my open mouth.

"Tia, my love. I am so sorry for the way I have treated you these last few weeks. I know it's not an excuse, but I think it took me so long to get over what happened because I care so deeply about you, and I had to be sure it was real. And it is. I love you more than life itself. Will you marry me?" Luke says.

Tears spring to my eyes and I nod.

"Of course I will marry you," I say.

Luke gets to his feet and fumbles a small, red velvet box from his pocket. He opens it and I gasp again. Inside the box is a large diamond sitting atop a golden band. The diamond is a solitaire cut, and I know straight away Luke asked Louisa to help with choosing the ring as well as setting this up, because I have shown her variations of this ring for years telling her it's my dream engagement ring.

Luke slips the ring onto my finger and then he looks into my eyes. I try to look back at him, but my own eyes are full of tears and he's just a blur of color. Luke leans down and kisses me and nothing else matters in that moment. I wrap my arms tightly around him like I never want to let go, and when we stop kissing, Luke keeps me in his arms and starts to waltz me slowly around the rooftop. I let him lead me and I lean back a bit so I can look up at his face.

"I will never lie to you again, I promise," I say. "I love you too, and this has made me the happiest woman alive."

"I'm glad you said the happiest woman and not the happiest person, because we would have had our first argument as an engaged couple if you'd said that, because I have already claimed that title," Luke says.

We kiss again and my body responds to Luke's kiss like it always has, only this time, I don't try to hold back when I feel the attachment and I realize something that I should have known all along. Being in Luke's embrace feels like coming home.

*Epilogue*

## TIA

Two Years Later

I'm kind of nervous as the celebrant calls upon Luke and me to come forward with our baby. What if she cries? Well, she's sure to cry, all babies do, but what if she won't stop? I tell myself to stop worrying and try to enjoy the moment. I get up and carry our baby forward,

"Welcome to the naming ceremony of Ebba Jackson," the celebrant says.

Luke and I both agreed we didn't want a religious service and we're doing this our way. The celebrant talks about life and the responsibilities of parents and then she talks about the importance of a name, and she explains how we are naming our baby after my Swedish mom.

"Luke, Tia, do you both promise to raise this child with

love and help her to become a valued part of her community?" the celebrant says.

"We do," Luke and I say.

The celebrant smiles and looks out over the room filled with family and friends. I look out there too and I see Luke's mom is beaming, and she catches my eye, and I smile back at her.

"Do you, the family and friends, promise to help Luke and Tia raise Ebba should they need your support?" the celebrant says.

"We do," the congregation says as one, and I can't stop the smile from crossing my face,

"Can we have Louisa Sanchez up here please," the celebrant says, and Louisa comes up to the front.

"Louisa, do you promise to be an aunt to Ebba, to be there for her whenever she should need you, and to support her parents with raising her with love?" the celebrant says.

"I do," Louisa says.

"And should any event occur, that should leave Ebba alone in this world, do you, Louisa, promise to take the child into your home and into your heart?" the celebrant says.

Of course, Luke and I have already discussed this with Louisa and asked her to be Ebba's guardian if anything should happen to us, but this still feels like a special moment to me, and I find that I'm holding my breath while I wait for Louisa to answer.

"I do," she says.

Her part done, Louisa goes and retakes her seat, and I hand Ebba to the celebrant. She's fine in the woman's arms, until the water is poured on her head, and she sniffles a little bit, but she soon settles back down, and I see that all of my worries were for nothing.

"In view of your family and friends, I officially name you Ebba Jackson. May all of your wishes and dreams come true dear child," the celebrant says, and she hands our baby back to me.

With the service over, our friends and family come up to take photographs of us and then they come closer and start congratulating us. Enrique makes everyone smile when he takes Ebba in his arms and beams proudly around the room.

"This is my surrogate granddaughter," he announces.

I love that despite me not having any blood relatives anymore, except Ebba of course, that I am still surrounded by love, and I know that no matter what the future holds for us, Luke and I will always have each other, and Ebba will never, ever be alone in this world.

"I love you," I say to Luke.

He smiles at me and kisses the top of my head.

"I love you too," he says. "More every day."


And they lived happily ever after…

*Coming soon...*

HARD BOSS

## Chapter One

### Juliette

Choosing a dress for my first day at work is proving to be unnecessarily difficult. It's a hard choice since it has to be something between simple and professional. I stare at myself in the mirror and take in the black suit I have on. I look okay in it, but it's a bit funereal and okay isn't what I'm going for this morning.

Today is a day of first impressions, and I really do want to make a good one. I want to get in, do my job, and return home. Repeat the same process for as long as it takes to gather all the money I need. Jenny says I might spend my first day meeting with other girls and that's okay. I'm not emotionally invested or looking for any opportunities here. I just need to make more money and save enough to start my bakery.

My job is simple. I'm what Jenny calls a replacement secretary. There are men who are too important to survive a day without an assistant, and should a case arise where their regular assistant or secretaries aren't available, they reach out to my agency to hire a secretary on rental. The job description is simple enough. I'm to perform all the tasks required of a secretary.

I should go for something chic and simple. A powder blue suit, very demure. My intention is to look like a ray of sunshine, approachable and friendly, but still interesting, given the slit that extends a couple of inches above my knees. I hope it's not too much. I certainly don't want to offend anybody. For makeup, I go light like I usually do. Anymore and I'll be too busy trying to keep from clawing my face off from the tingling.

There, I'm ready for my first day at work!

Filled with excitement and intense anxiety I start the commute over. I really need this to work. I need the money so badly. The drive takes about thirty minutes, and Jenny is there to welcome me.

"Juliette, I'm glad you could make it," she says and pulls me into a hug as she leads me down the hall to join the other girls. It really helps to settle my nerves and is just what I need.

There are about six of them in an open office area and Jenny tells me they are all waiting on a call to serve as a short-term secretary. If today is a busy day, Jenny says we will all be out of the building in an hour. But she is pretty sure it won't be. I hope it is because the contract I signed, while I get a base fee, is based on commission. The more jobs I get, the higher my commission.

Juliette introduces me to the other girls, and it quickly becomes obvious that I have much to learn. I sit quietly and listen attentively to the girls talk, looking to see if I can make friends with any of them. They talk about their recent encounters with some of the bosses and complain about some bosses that are a pain in the ass to work with.

"All I'm saying is basic decency requires you address me by my name and not whistle to call me," one of the girls says with a shake of her head. "I have a name. It's Tessa. Call it."

Jenny excuses herself to get to work and I move closer to the girls so I can join in on their conversation.

"Hi, I'm Kendra," one of the girls introduces herself and then the other girls introduce themselves. I try to remember all of their names because they'll be colleagues for as long as I remain with the agency, and I know I need to form a good rapport with them.

"Hey everybody. My name is Juliette," I reply and ask a question that has been bothering me. "It isn't always like that, is it? You get decent bosses sometimes?"

"You get decent ones most times. They come in different flavors, but most of them are too busy to notice you. Some can be so stressed they are stuck in rude mode. You'll learn to tolerate and handle each of them very quickly. None of us plan to be here forever. It is just temporary. I'm doing this to put myself through college," Kendra says. She can tell I'm already worried about working with the kind of bosses Tessa just described. However, if anyone can handle such bosses, it's me.

This is consoling feedback. I don't tell her I plan on saving enough to open my bakery. I have a tangible amount saved already and if the payment scheme Jenny shared with me is correct, I'll need to do about eighty to a hundred gigs to get enough money to open my bakery. That is roughly a year's worth of work.

Jenny returns after a while and helps me through the registration process. After the registration, I join the other girls at the open office. The number has increased in the short time I was with Jenny. Having no intention of excluding myself, I join them and introduce myself to the newcomers. Some are cordial, a couple are cold, and a few are nonchalant.

I don't really care. No emotional attachments, I remind myself. I have a goal, and this is all I should put my focus on.

Most of the girls get called to places that have requested them. I have no choice but to wait. After about an hour of waiting, Jenny comes outside with a folder in hand.

"We have a last-minute gig that has just come in," she announces, and the handful of us look up at in her.

"Who is it?" one of the girls asks.

"Aliya has called in sick."

"Again?" Kendra groans.

"Oh, I'm sure she is sick. Sick of his ass, no doubt," another girl says, and the other murmur in agreement.

I'm lost here, but I guess this is one of the bosses Tessa was talking about.

"Am I assuming there are no takers?" Jenny asks.

The girls look blandly at Jenny. I get the message. This is my chance to get my first job. But why are the others reluctant and unwilling to work with this man?

"Who is Aliya?" I ask Kendra.

"The right question is who is her boss," Kendra says.

"Hudson Sinclair," Susan, a petite red-head provides the answer. I catch the resentment in her voice.

"You don't want to be working for him, dear. And definitely not as your first gig," Tessa adds.

"Why not?"

"He's an asshole, is why," Susan explains. "He is a perfectionist to the letter. Difficult to work with and his assistant Aliya is always calling in sick. We all think she calls in sick whenever she doesn't want to put up with his bullshit."

"If it were me, that'll be every day," one of the girls mutters.

"He can't be that bad," I say.

"Oh, he's worse," Susan says tartly. "I made the mistake of working for him three weeks ago because I needed the commission. The worst day of my life. I counted down the minutes until my time was over."

Hudson Sinclair sounds like someone I should avoid, but beggars can't be choosy. A plan is fomenting in my mind. If Hudson has an assistant who calls in sick consistently, he must be a regular here and if no one is willing to take up his gig, it'll always be available for me.

"How often does Aliya get sick?" I ask.

"Maybe once or twice a month," Tessa answers my question.

They are all looking at me now, wondering if I will be crazy enough to risk working for Hudson Sinclair on my first day at work.

An average of five times a month gives me sixty gigs assured in the year. Couple that with other gigs I'll pick up along the line, and I'll hit the hundred mark and get the big bonus, which will be more than enough money to start my bakery.

Susan shakes her head with disbelief. "You really aren't thinking of doing it? You'll be crazy to."

"What's life without a little craziness?" I ask and pick up my bag, heading towards Jenny.

"I knew you'd say yes," Jenny says with a cheeky grin. "You never could resist a challenge."

"The other girls think I'm being a fool."

"Do you want the truth from me?" she asks with arched eyebrows.

"Go for it."

"Will it change your mind?"

"I don't think so," I reply.

"Good. They're right. Sinclair is a repeat client. He is terrible to work with and will constantly keep you on your toes. Nothing you do is ever good enough for him, and you shouldn't expect even the slightest bit of appreciation from him. It's like you don't exist to him. But we keep him because he pays well."

"Even if he's an inconvenience to the girls?"

"We try not to force him on any of the girls. We let them decide to work with him. The last two calls he made for a secretary were left unanswered because we were unable to assist him as no one was willing to work with him. We've explained to him why that is so, but he is unwilling to change."

"He sounds like a terrible person."

Jenny cocks her head and then shakes it. "He isn't terrible per se. I've worked with him when I was still a temp. He is straightforward and curt. If you try to stick to his rules, you won't get into any trouble with him. Of course, you won't enjoy the work, but are you here to enjoy it?"

I get the message.

"Alright. What do I need to know about the job?"

"It involves traveling," Jenny says. "So, it is a high-paying commission, and we don't know how long it'll last. He has left the contract open-ended. Of course, you're free to break it off at any time. But I'll advise you not to. You'll forfeit the bonus that should come with such a lengthy gig."

"So, I'm going to work with a man no one is willing to work with for an unspecified length of time, and your best advice is for me to leave unless the time expires."

"Pretty much," Jenny shrugs.

"This should be fun," I say and relax. The others might have bad reviews for Mr. Sinclair, but I intend to have a good time working for him. It might not be enjoyable, as Jenny pointed out, but it won't be miserable.

I complete the required paperwork, and Jenny orders me an Uber to drive me to the office. Back in the open office, the other girls tell me they think I'm crazy. Kendra calls me cuckoo. When we arrive at the building, I walk up to the receptionist at the front desk and explain who I am to her.

"Are you new?" she asks me.

"Yes."

She gives me the direction to Hudson Sinclair's office. As the elevator takes me up to the floor his office is on, I have half the mind to stop the elevator, ride it back down and return to Jenny and tell her I changed my mind.

Jenny wouldn't begrudge me of the choice, I'm certain.

But I have never been one to chicken out of a tough situation. When life gives you lemons, you throw them into a blender and make lemonade. I get to the office and knock on the door. A husky voice calls from behind the door.

"Come in," it says.

I open the door and find a man busy at work on his laptop. Without looking at me he groans.

"They found someone for me," he mutters. "I wonder if this one will be any good."

Enjoy the rest of the book
by pre-ordering here:
Hard Boss

## About the Author

Thank you so much for reading!
If you have enjoyed the book and would like to leave a
precious review for me, please kindly do so here:

It's Only Make Believe

Please click on the link below to receive info about my latest
releases and giveaways.
<u>NEVER MISS A THING</u>

Or
come say 'hello' here:

_Also by Jona Rose_

Dream Crusher

Until He Confesses

Insufferable Boss

Strictly Business

Confessing To The CEO

Enemy Boss

The Bride's Brother

The Bet

One Bossy Night

Not Yet Yours

Surviving the Boss